Three's the Charm

By Chloe Cocking

Filidh Publishing

First Softcover Printing: 2021
ISBN 978-1-927848-72-2
Filidh Publishing
www.filidhbooks.com

Cover photograph

 CC0 Public Domain

Free for personal and commercial use

No attribution required Learn more

Cover design by Danny Weeds

*To the New Westminster writers,
for laughing in all the right places.*

To Rob, just because.

Table of Contents

Persephone and the Imp

Persephone and the Imp

Chapter One

"She's done what?!" Thirteen-year-old Persephone slapped her forehead as she listened to her friend and familiar, Dap the imp.

Dap fidgeted as he perched on Persephone's lap and licked his lips. His twenty-centimetre-long tongue was more than adequate for the job. Dap's entire face received a moist, haphazard daubing.

Persephone reassured her small imp by gently scratching him behind the ears. "I'm not mad at you, Dap, just . . . surprised that Mother would do such a thing." Persephone felt the tension in the imp's body recede. His skin started to warm and return to its usual mottled red-and-black colour.

"Mistress, all the imps are talking about it. Their witches fear starvation, and they've had to return to the Underworld. Humans will die, too."

"I guess the return of witches would explain the long lines outside of Hades' reception room."

She shuddered. She did not like to spend time near the Lord of the Underworld, even in his best moods. Persephone had observed that the increased number of petitioners made Hades even more irritable and petty than usual. She did her best to stay out of his way.

"Dap, sweetling, can you perch on my shoulder, please? I want to stand and pace. I think better when I pace."

Dap leapt gracefully to the young goddess' shoulder and settled himself, wrapping his long scaly tail around her neck like a torc. Persephone stood, adjusted the skirt of her embroidered gown, and started to pace the length of her obsidian cave.

"You smell worried," Dap observed.

"I am. You say soon humans will be dying from lack of food because Mother is threatening to make the land fallow, that even the rich will quickly deplete their stores of grain. When no humans are sacrificing grain and animals to the Gods, the Gods will starve, too."

"Do you think they will war amongst themselves?" Dap asked as he clung more tightly around Persephone's neck.

Dap was grateful to Persephone; unlike most imps, he had not been assigned to a witch on Earth as a familiar. He was much smaller and weaker than his kind usually were. The Lord of Underworld saw no reason to give special privileges to weaklings, so Dap had been friendless in the Underworld until Persephone saw him and claimed him as her own.

"I think they'll kill my Mother and replace her with another Goddess. Or perhaps slaughter any remaining humans and start the world anew."

Dap's muscles stiffened in alarm. "We don't want that!"
Persephone raised her left hand and stroked the part of Dap's tail that curled against her collarbone.
Her strides lengthened, and the obsidian floor rang with the staccato taps of her boot heels. Dap could almost hear her mind working, stretching toward a solution.

"Hhmm, so here's what we know: if Mother won't let crops grow until Hades returns me to her, eventually the Gods will kill her. But on the other hand, if I have to spend the rest of my existence in the Underworld with that creep, Hades, I don't think I will be able to survive."

Dap shivered. Since Hades had kidnapped Persephone, the Lord of the Underworld had been on his best behaviour. If she didn't soon agree to marry Hades, Dap feared for her.

In response to her imp's shivering, Persephone stopped pacing and took a deep breath, calming them both. "I think we'll have to compromise. I don't want to, but I don't see any other way."

Dap lifted his ears, and the tip of his tail twitched against Persephone's clavicle. "How?" he asked.

"What if we tell Hades that I'll become his queen if he promises that for six months of the year I can stay with Mother?"

Dap sniffed, the pointed end of his nose twitching. "How does that help?

"Well, I think I can convince Mother to end her strike for the months I am with her. That should give the humans enough time to gather and preserve extra food so they have something to eat when I am away from her in the Underworld. They'll also set aside a portion to use as sacrifices to the gods."

"Hhm, I could put word out to other imps that they need to tell their witches about this, and start getting ready to preserve food. The witches can tell the humans . . .

"If they listen." Persephone started to pace again.

Dap chuckled. "Even humans are smart enough to listen to witches sometimes. That way you'll save at least some of the humans, enough to keep the gods fed, anyway."

"So how do we get Hades to agree?" Persephone rubbed her chin as she thought. "I could tell him that even if we are married, when I'm with Mother, he need not be faithful to me."

The last thing Persephone wanted was Hades' sexual attention; she had seen how he carried on during feasts.

Dap smirked, the loose folds of skin on his face deepening into furrows. "Whatever he does in the Underworld stays in the Underworld?"

Persephone nodded. "I think we should really dress it up for him, too. You know how much he loves ritual. Maybe we could make a big deal out of the number six? Six of something to symbolize the six months I will be with Demeter?"

Dap thought for a moment, talons gripping the fabric of Persephone's dress. "What if you ate six of something in front of him and the whole court? Make a performance of it, really ham it up, give him a good show."

"And stress to him that by agreeing to the compromise his brothers are going to owe him one . . ."

Dap bounced on her shoulder, "Yes, exactly! Get him from both sides—he gets to cheat on his soon-to-be wife, consequence-free, for six months of every year, all while looking like a magnanimous big shot." Dap's mottled tail lashed with excitement.

"Let's do it!" Persephone said. "Shall we toast to it?"

"Certainly," Dap replied as he leapt from her shoulder. "I'll go get us some wine; we've got something to celebrate."

Persephone smiled at her familiar as he scampered away.

She thought, "Something to celebrate, and much more to scheme."

Chapter Two

Hades had been surprised when his young captive niece, Persephone, had begged a private audience with him. Since the day he pulled her by the hair into his flaming chariot and dragged her to the Underworld, she had barely spoken to him. Sometimes he could feel her eyes on him from across the Great Hall when he required her to be in attendance. Her cool, unwavering gaze unnerved him.

Over the past six months, he had often wondered how a girl not even worthy of the name "goddess" unsettled him so. It wasn't that he was worried about the girl's harridan of a mother.

Demeter's petulant threats would backfire on her soon enough, and the gods would make a replacement earth goddess. They had done it before, when the last one had gotten out of line. Hades did not care if mere humans and witches died; indeed, it was better for him if they did, as it meant the population of the Underworld increased, and Hades' powers along with it. Still, more subjects would mean more work. Hades was ambivalent about that. He liked to feast, and drink, and chase pretty girls and boys into his bed. Administrative duties got in the way of his preferred pastimes.

He let Persephone stew for a few days before he deigned to respond to her request.

At first, he thought he might tell her that all private time with him must involve sex, just to get the girl to submit. When he spoke to his consul Mim about this, the wizened imp had cautioned him.

"She is still young, only thirteen human years. She will be at least thirty human years before we can assess the extent of her goddess powers and domains of protection," Mim said.

Hades shrugged. "So what?"

Mim sighed. "Goddesses hold grudges, your Majesty. If you force her now, she will make you pay for that when she fully comes into her powers."

"If she can . . ."

"Majesty, is that really a risk you want to take? Her father is Zeus, after all. She could manifest . . . anything. Best not to antagonize her. You know what they say: 'happy wife, happy life.'"

Hades had not known how to respond to that. He resented being told "no" by any being.

However, eventually his curiosity was so great he granted Persephone a private audience without any caveats. Just to prove that he sometimes actually took Mim's advice, Hades invited the elderly imp to be in attendance.

At the appointed time, Persephone arrived in Hades' personal chambers, accompanied by Dap.

Hades thought, "I wish she wouldn't drag that that scrawny runt whatshisname around with her everywhere. Dab? Sap? . . . I can't even remember her pathetic pet's name. No matter."

Out loud he said, "Sit, girl, and tell me what is so important you must trouble me with it."

She sat in the chair opposite Hades; her wrinkled Dap curled up on her lap like a cat. She stroked him with light fingertips.

He thought, "How can she bear to touch such . . . weakness?"

Hades felt his gorge rise. "Mim's probably wrong about her—only the weak can tolerate the company of the weak." He felt an impulse to roll his eyes, but restrained himself. "If people only knew the sacrifices I make for their comfort," he thought.

Hades cleared his throat and said, "Mim, wine, now."

Mim poured wine red as blood into jewelled cups, then crouched near Hades' feet.

As Hades sipped, he noted that Persephone seemed to have taken great care with her appearance. She wore a golden velvet dress with tiny diamonds scattered across the skirt and bodice. Her dark hair hung in loose waves to her waist. Her clear green eyes looked round and innocent, with nothing of the usual disdain.

Persephone smiled at Hades like the sun coming out from behind a cloud. "Majesty, thank you for granting me this audience. I am too shy to declare my heart in front of everyone in the great hall." She glanced at him through her lashes; they lay like fine dark lace against her cheeks.

Hades felt something stir in his loins. He ignored the sensation. "Time for that later," he thought. Out loud he said, "Well?"

Persephone stroked the imp on her lap. "I think . . . I think . . . I am ready to marry you."

Hades cocked his head to one side. He glanced down at Mim, who was so expressionless that he may as well have been carved from stone. He resisted the urge to nudge Mim with his boot. Hades cleared his throat. "Good. You have come to your senses. When?"

"Majesty, my imp informs that the thirteenth of this month is the most auspicious day for our wedding."

"She is correct, sir," Mim said. "It is particularly auspicious as the thirteenth of this month is also the thirteenth full moon of the year."

Hades glanced at his consul. "Can a feast and all the finery be readied in just five days?"

"Anything you command shall be so," Mim replied.

"Fine, it shall be so."

Persephone sighed. Hades noticed how the candlelight gleamed on the pale skin of her décolletage as she did so. "It's hard to believe my niece is only thirteen," he thought. He shifted in his chair.

"I must ask one small boon of you, Majesty. It can be your bridegroom's gift to me if you like."

"Out with it."

"Please, I would like to invite my mother to the wedding feast."

Hades scowled. Persephone's hands shook as she stroked Dap's scaly skin.

"Your Majesty, if I may . . ." Mim stood to attention besides Hades' chair.

"You may."

"This would be an excellent act of diplomacy, considering . . . everything," said Mim.

Hades looked from Mim's wizened visage to his young bride-to-be's apple-green eyes. They were glossy with tears.

Hades heaved an irritated sigh, drained his cup of wine with a practiced twist of his wrist, and said, "Fine, fine, invite her, Mim."

Persephone smiled beatifically and continued to stroke her dozing imp.

Chapter Three

For the next five days, the Underworld buzzed as all its denizens were pressed into service under Mim's watchful eye. One group of souls worked together to create matching embroidered garments for bride and bridegroom. Another group made pastries and cakes to feed the expected crowd. A third group of souls walked the Earth, hunting wild birds and game. When they returned to the Underworld, they roasted huge joints of meat and entire pheasants over slow fires, basting all the while.

Mim released hundreds of ravens to carry wedding invitations to gods and goddesses, socially prominent witches, the high priest of Hades' temple at Elis and all his acolytes, and even a few very wealthy humans who had curried favour with Hades.

Mim took extra care with the ravens he dispatched with Demeter's invitation. The larger of the two birds was tasked with carrying a basket of pomegranates, a peace offering from Hades to his future mother-in-law. The smaller bird carried the formal invitation in her beak, along with a letter in Persephone's own hand. The letter explained how Persephone had come to love Hades and was marrying him of her own free will. Mim took care to check the letter for any codes, invisible ink, or small enchantments. He did not entirely trust the young goddess's change of heart.

So many ravens were coming and going; no one noticed small Dap sending out a few ravens of his own.

Chapter Four

The morning of the wedding, Persephone sat before a mirror in her cave, candlelight gleaming off the ebon walls. She allowed souls to arrange her hair, wash and perfume her body, and dress her. She was uncomfortable with this. Demeter's court was simple, a sunny cottage that smelled of freshly-baked bread and strawberries. No one had handmaidens.

Persephone was also aware that any attendants were likely to be spies—some sent by Hades, some by Mim, some by parties as yet unknown. She did not want her hair brushed by spies. But there was no way to dismiss them on her wedding day without raising eyebrows and questions. Persephone was a practical young goddess, so she swallowed her discomfort and acquiesced, for now.

Dap perched on a velvet-tufted stool, handing hair pins and flower buds to the hairdressing souls, threading needles for the souls who were sewing Persephone into her gown, and fetching water or wine for any who asked. He seemed excited about the preparations: his mottled black-and-red hide was a deep garnet, the imp equivalent to a human's flush.

Persephone was silent, by design. She knew that the less she said, the less could be reported, the less would need to be denied or explained later. She held very still, allowing the souls to flutter around her. She sipped only water, and waited.

At ten minutes before midnight—the designated time for the feast, for in the Underworld feasting always came before a ceremony—Dap settled a veil as thin as smoke over Persephone. He fixed it to the back of her head so it cascaded down over her river of hair. Then he climbed down from his tall stool and stood beside her as she regarded herself in her mirror.

14

"Are you ready?" Dap asked.

"As I'll ever be," Persephone said, voice soft.

"I won't ride on your shoulder. It will ruin the presentation. But I can carry your train, if you like."

"That would be excellent, thank you." Persephone's eyes were brimming and glossy because of this small act of kindness. She fanned them to dry her tears.

She dismissed the last few souls from her chambers. Without speaking, lest they be overhead, Dap crawled under Persephone's bed and returned with a drawstring canvas bag. He handed it to her, and she removed items: a scrap of parchment, a sharp silver blade, and a golden pomegranate. She handed the scrap of parchment to Dap and he buttoned it securely in his vest pocket. Both paused for a moment to admire the blade and the pomegranate; they gleamed as Persephone turned them over in her hands. Witches on earth had crafted these items for her, to use in place of a sceptre and orb. She admired their cunning work: the pomegranate felt and smelled like a natural fruit despite how it looked.

"The witches did well," she thought.

She smiled at Dap, nodded.

They left Persephone's chamber. The walk to the great hall would be slow due to Dap's short legs, but their way was lit by the glow shivering off the knife and fruit.

When they reached the Great Hall, they paused on the threshold. Everyone was seated and drinking wine. Musicians played theremins and chimes from a dais.

She scanned the crowd for Demeter or anyone from Demeter's court.

"Not here yet," Persephone thought. "That's fine. There is plenty of time".

She noticed that a seat at the high table had been prepared for Demeter, with flowers and sheaves of grain decorating her place.

"Mim does lovely work," she thought.

The only other empty chair at the high table was the one next to Hades, a single black rosebud laid in the center of the golden plate.

When Hades saw his young bride-to-be enter, he stood up and clapped his hands. The guests' chatter died down to a mere murmur.

"Welcome, my dear." His voice boomed. "Come sit next to me."

Persephone tightened her fingers around the handle of her silver knife, but she raised her gaze, smiled broadly at Hades, displayed her dimples.

"Yes, my lord," she said, dipping a shallow curtsy. She could feel the eyes of her other uncle, Poseidon, on her face.

"Ugh, it's like he can bore holes with his stares," she thought as she swallowed her irritation. "And Zeus is absent from the table entirely, absentee father to the very last. I'm marrying his brother, my uncle—you'd think he'd find a way to show up for that. But I suppose he's busy turning himself into a shower of gold and raping shepherdesses. When is he not?"

Persephone repressed a shrug. She scanned the crowd, brow furrowed. "And where is Mother?" Her panic started to rise. "Where is she?" she thought.

From the far end of the hall there was a great clatter. A murmur moved through the crowd like a wave. The guests parted, leaving a wide pathway. At its far end stood Demeter. She had entered from the kitchen.

Demeter was barefoot, crowned with sheaves of woven wheat, wearing a dress made of simple linen homespun. Her dark blonde hair was in two long plaits, the ends of which hung to her knees. She had no attendants, and carried no weapon, just a lantern she had used to navigate the service tunnels in the Underworld.

"Daughter," she said, her voice mellifluous as dark honey. "I am so glad to see you."
The thirteen-year-old girl in Persephone felt great relief at the sight of Demeter. She wanted to run, sobbing, into her mother's arms. She wanted to collapse against Demeter's warm body, safe from harm.

But Persephone, the emerging politician, knew she must not. She took a deep breath, steadying her nerves. She tilted her head in a slight bow towards her mother, retrieved her train from

Dap, and moved swiftly to Hades' side. The crowd—denied the scene they had expected—resumed their chatter.

Dap waddled to Demeter so he could lead the unaccompanied goddess to the great table.

When Demeter was seated, and Dap had scurried under Persephone's chair—the best place to avoid any careless or arrogant booted feet—Hades raised his cup.

"Let the feast begin!" he cried.

Chapter Five

"Wait! Wait for a moment!" Persephone begged.

The theremins and chimes went silent, as did the crowd.

"Sir, a boon on my wedding day, I beseech you!"

"I thought your boon was an invitation to your mother," Hades spat the last word like it was a wad of phlegm.

Persephone smiled into his face, then lowered her lashes.

"I am but a young girl, moved by many enthusiasms," she said, voice breathy.

"Come on, Hades," said Poseidon, leering, "Grant the girl another boon; she'll be granting you one soon enough."

The skin around Demeter's eyes tightened, but she remained silent, hands in her lap.

Persephone willed tears into her eyes, and was amazed that such a thing came so easily.

Hades heaved the sigh of the oppressed. "Fine, yes, silly girl, what shall you have now?"

"Just this." She raised her hand, proffering the golden pomegranate. "It came by messenger with a note this morning, from one of the priests at your temple on Elis. He could not be here today, but sent this as a gift."
"And?"

"And the note said that the pomegranate holds six enchanted seeds. They hold the secret to us having a fulfilling marriage, if I swallow the seeds before the wedding banquet begins. That blessing is his gift to us, but it will only work if we follow his instructions."

"Oh?"

"The note said you must be the one to feed them to me; if it is done that way, our marriage can never be sundered, not even by gods-death."

"Interesting . . . but before I do anything: why do you want this?" Hades said, eyebrow cocked.

Persephone looked startled; her moist pink lips were parted, her eyes twin green pools of surprise. A blush crept up her neck and across her cheeks "It's romantic. Imagine a bond that cannot be broken! I love you! I want our marriage to be perfect!"

Hades chuckled. He thought of the dozens of wives he'd had in his long existence. Human women did not survive with long with him. His amorous attentions were too vigorous. Even witches could not withstand his attentions for more than a year or two. He'd never wedded a near-immortal goddess before, let alone bedded one.

"She will be mine forever, or until I get bored," he thought. Something about that idea pleased him.

Poseidon broke in. "Hades, damn your eyes, I am starving, and my loins are a-twitch. Give our silly niece the seeds she wants so we can get on the feasting and such."

He squeezed the buttock of one of the souls who had died young and comely. She twisted away from him, almost spilling the pitcher of wine she was carrying.

Mim appeared at Hades' elbow. "Sire, how do we know what the girl says is true? How do we know the pomegranate came from Elis?"

Dap scurried from underneath Persephone's chair and handed a scrap of parchment to the elder imp. Mim wrinkled his nose as his eyes, and sixth sense scanned the note for any enchantments, traces of poison.

At last, Mim pronounced, "This appears to be in order, Your Majesty." He bowed his head and stepped back from the high table.

"The pomegranate has an Elis makers-mark on it," Persephone said, turning the fruit over in her hand to display it.

Hades snatched it from her and peered at it. "Yes, I see the mark. Let us proceed."

"You're supposed to cut it with this knife in particular; it is part of the ceremony," she said, offering him the handle of the silver blade.

Hades placed the fruit on the plate at his place at the table. He cleaved the golden sphere neatly in two.

He peered at the contents. It was empty except for six garnet beads in the shape of pomegranate seeds. They glittered in the candlelight.

Addressing the crowd, Hades intoned, "This company gathered here tonight is my witness. She freely eats what I have given her with my own hand, so that our marriage can never be sundered!" With these last words, he glanced at Demeter, smirking.

Demeter sat at her place at the table, stoic, unmoving.

"Tilt your head back and open your mouth. I'll drop them in one by one."

Persephone did as she was bid.

Hades dropped the glossy red beads onto Persephone's tongue, one by one, giving her time to swallow each of them. He grabbed Persephone by the shoulders, lifting her to tip-toe, and kissed her mouth, sealing their fate. His kiss was so hard it split the plump pink cushion of her lower lip.

"Now, let the feasting begin!" proclaimed Hades.

Many imps and dead souls scurried around, offering great platters of roasted meat and fowl. Persephone shredded some pheasant breast on her plate to make it look as though she was eating. She slipped pieces to Dap for him to eat as he crouched under her chair. She wanted to keep her stomach empty, to give the seeds a chance to do their work. She noticed Poseidon had already gobbled up the food on his plate, and was calling for more wine as he tried to tumble a reluctant witch onto silken pillows heaped into one corner. Ten minutes into the banquet, and he must start the orgy already? She rolled her eyes, but no one noticed except for Demeter. Demeter allowed herself a tight little smile in her daughter's direction. She knew what was coming.

Just when Persephone was starting to fear something had gone wrong with the magic, she caught a whiff of an odour. There it is. She reached under her chair and squeezed Dap's tiny hand.

At first, Hades' didn't notice the smell. It was early in the feast, yes, but he was already drunk and distracted by his plans for Persephone's defloration.

He thought, "I've waited long enough for this, so I shall have her on this very table, right after the ceremony. Should I have it cleared first? No, I am Lord of Underworld, so I will take her on a table littered with bones while everyone watches. If she kicks over a jug of gravy while she struggles, what of it? Then I might offer her to the highest bidder, just for the sport of it. Just not Poseidon; I'm not sharing with my damn brother anymore."

As he sucked the marrow from a segment of venison rib, Hades felt a ripple of nausea trill up his esophagus. "Something smells. Something smells bad," he thought. He put the half-sucked rib down on his plate, and wiped his greasy hands on his embroidered velvet trousers.

Standing beside Hades' chair, Mim frowned, thinking of the expense and imp-hours that went into the trousers' construction.

Hades lifted each of his arms in turn, sniffing. He thought, "It's not me."

With thumb and forefinger, he picked up the rib from his plate and sniffed. "Not the meat, either," he thought. He turned to Mim.

"Do you smell that?" Hades said.

Mim cocked an eyebrow and sniffed a few times with his hooked nose. Mouth downturned at both corners, Mim nodded.

"What is it? It's disgusting!"

Mim nodded as a look of panic swept over his wrinkled face. He got only three steps away from Hades before Mim vomited.

Hades jumped up from his seat. He pointed at one of the dead souls standing at attention nearby. "You, clean that up!" Gesturing at other servants, "You two, take Mim to his quarters."

Persephone, meek, eyes downcast, took a small sip of her wine. The movement of her sleeve stirred the air.

The odour wafted from her, and caught Hades full in the face. He blanched, but his eyes blazed. He turned to her, caught her under the armpit, dragged her to standing.

"It's you!" he screamed, sniffing her hair, her neck, even burying his face in Persephone's bosom. He vomited all over her and the high table, spasms so severe he was forced to let go of her and grab the back of his chair to keep his balance.

By now, the stench had circulated. The unfortunate witch pinned under Poseidon on the silken cushions vomited a thick green paste into his face. He leapt off her, trousers around his ankles.

"My stars, woman, what did you eat?" he shouted.

Another volley of vomit arced from the witch's mouth, this time splattering Poseidon from his belly to his knees. Something about seeing vomit dripping from his still-erect penis was more than Poseidon could endure, so he threw up near-endless waves of red wine onto the stone floor.

Now everyone near the high table in the great hall was vomiting helplessly. Imps, witches, dead souls, gods and goddesses, all of them—for the moment anyway—reduced to mere meat hanging off a spasming tube with a mind of its own. Everyone who smelled the terrible odour seeping from Persephone's pores was afflicted—everyone but Dap, Demeter, and Persephone herself.

Hades, sitting backwards on his chair, rested his sweaty forehead against the velvet backrest.

Voice low, Hades said, "You've done something." He turned his head so he could spray vomit off to one side.
Wiping his mouth on his black lace shirt cuff, he said again, "You've done something."
Persephone leaned over and patted Hades' shoulder. "Darling one, I am so sorry to see you become ill. Is the wine vinegar? Is the meat foul?"

Her proximity intensified the smell. Hades moaned, and vomited blood this time. His entire GI tract, from lips to anus, clenched.

"Just get out," he said. More loudly: "Do you hear me, Demeter?" He vomited more blood. "Take this little bitch and get out!"

"My love, I don't understand, don't you want me?"

"Get out!"

Demeter stood up from her place at the end of the high table. To the assembled company too far away to have been rendered ill, Demeter boomed, "Leave while you can, pass through the kitchens." Her voice echoed against the obsidian walls of the great hall.

The as-yet-unafflicted ran for the kitchens. The afflicted writhed and spewed. Persephone took Dap by the hand, and quickly sponged him clean. Even hidden under Persephone's chair, he'd endured some back spray.

"Dap, sweetling, can we leave your vest behind? I am afraid it is ruined."

"Yes," he said, shrugging off the soiled garment, "but what of your gown?"
"I never want to see it again after tonight."

Demeter said, "Hurry now, children, I have fresh clothes for you, just outside the mouth of Underworld. There is a spring there where you can bathe."

Dap undid the lacings of Persephone's gown. Stiff with boning, embroidery, and drying vomit, she shrugged it to the floor. The bodice stood upright of its own accord. Persephone stepped out of that confinement, and lifted Dap to her shoulder. His talons were gentle on her bare skin, for he could brace himself by wrapping his tail around her upper arm.

Demeter, while far less soiled than Dap and Persephone, was still dirtier than she could tolerate. She pulled her long shift off over her head and tossed it over the lake of multi-coloured vomit swirling between them and the kitchen door. She adjusted the flame on her lantern.

"Let's away, no time to waste."

The two naked goddesses, one with a small naked imp on her shoulder, ran for the kitchen doors.

Chapter Six

Persephone sat cross-legged on the front porch of her mother's small stone cottage, worrying and watching Helios' chariot paint the clouds orange and pink as he completed the last of this day's journey across the heavens. Dap was curled into a tight circle on her lap, long pointed ears folded over his eyes like a sleeping mask. He was snoring softly.

Demeter was just a few meters away, standing in the front garden of her home, surrounded by flowers and fruit trees. With the help of two imp retainers, she was accepting grain tributes from humans and witches. She had been doing so since dawn, and would continue through twilight until full dark. There were many people in line, waiting to give their tithe. Demeter blessed every person, no matter how small their contributions. This made the line move slowly, but neither goddess nor tributees seemed to mind. A faint herbaceous perfume hung over the entire property—a nature spell, Demeter's specialty, intended to soothe anyone in line who grew impatient.

Today was the last day of Thesmophoria, the harvest festival. Tomorrow Persephone would return to the Underworld for the first time since her wedding to Hades. Despite the pervasive calm engendered by the nature spell, Persephone was anxious.

"I wonder how I'd feel if Mother wasn't using a nature spell? I'm ready to climb out of my own skin as it is," she thought.

Cradling the still-sleeping Dap against her abdomen, Persephone stood up and started to pace. "I always think better when I pace."

She looked at the sky, no longer kissed with fire. "Mother has only another twenty minutes or so until full dark; she will finish soon."

Persephone walked back and forth across the grass in front of her mother's house, waiting. Fireflies zig-zagged around the last few people in line, but their tiny lights were dim in comparison to the rosy glow that wreathed Demeter's head. Finally, Demeter accepted the offering of the last witch in line. She blessed the witch, gave her the kiss of peace, and announced, "Thesmophoria is complete for this year. The land has been harvested!"

Demeter clapped her hands, and the pink light of her halo faded to nothing. The herbaceous scent of Demeter's nature spell dissipated.

She turned to Persephone and said, "Thank you for your patience, Daughter. Let's eat and speak together before Mim comes."

"Mim is coming?" Persephone felt her stomach lurch at the thought. Dap, sensing her fear even though he slept, roused himself and sat up straight.

"What's happening? Why do you smell afraid?" Dap asked.

"Mother says Mim is on his way," Persephone said.

Dap's forehead winkled.

"Nothing to fear from a practical old imp like him. Come inside and eat," said Demeter.

The three went inside and ate soup and bread. Dap cleared the dishes, then perched on Persephone's shoulder, tail coiled around her throat.

"So Mim comes because I have invited him," said Demeter.

"Mother, why?" Persephone's eyes were round, brows raised.

"Late last night he sent a raven with a letter. He asked for a chance to brief you before you returned to the Underworld. It seemed prudent to me to do so."

Persephone nodded, scowling. "I know, you are right. I keep hoping there is some way to wiggle out of this, though." Dap stroked her cheek with the curved side of his talons, tender as a mother with a newborn babe. His ears perked, swivelling in all directions.

"I can hear him," Dap said, pointing with one knobby mottled finger toward the pathway the celebrants had been using all day.

Demeter glanced at her right hand, balled in a fist. It started to glow with silver light. She flicked her fist in that direction with an effortless twist of the wrist.
"Battle magic, Mother?" asked Persephone, fearing the worse.
Demeter laid a calming hand on her daughter's forearm.

"No, child, just a whip-o-will to light his way. Mim is old, and his eyes are not as sharp nor his footfalls as steady as they once were."

Persephone nodded.

Mim tottered into view, using a gnarled stick to walk. His back was bent and he was muttering to himself.

Seeing the elder imp's gait and posture, Demeter whispered, "Dap, please heat water for willow bark tea; Mim has need of it."

Putting her arm around Persephone's shoulders, Demeter added, "And some chamomile-honey tea for Persy, she looks like she could use it."

Dap skittered over to the kitchen fireplace and set a kettle of water on to boil. By the time the tea was ready, Mim had mounted the porch. He was huffing and puffing from the effort.

"Welcome to our home, Mim the imp," Demeter said. "Be welcome and be at peace."
Mim bowed, then stood up and mopped his sweating brow with an enormous pink silk handkerchief pulled from his left sleeve.

The four moved inside and sat at the kitchen table. Dap had already set the tea at their places.
Mim sniffed at his cup, frowning.

"What's this?"

"Willow bark tea. It tastes terrible, but will help your pain."

Mim raised his eyebrows but sipped anyway. Grimacing, he said, "You're quite correct about the first part, Madam. Let us hope the rest of what you say is also truthful." Mim mopped the sheen from his bald pate with his handkerchief and sipped again.

"My daughter does not know your situation, so cannot guess why you asked to come. Perhaps you can recount the events."

Mim took a third sip and settled into his chair in anticipation of a long discourse. Persephone noticed Mim sat a little straighter, and some of the tension around his slightly bulging eyes had eased.

"The tea is working. Good," she thought.

Mim cleared his throat. "Well, Madam, as I indicated, several hours after you three left Hades' great hall, all the retching and vomiting stopped. For about half of the afflicted, there was additional . . . bodily purging."

Persephone raised a brow in question. Dap leapt to her shoulder and whispered, "I think he means that many of those present shat themselves." Persephone suppressed a giggle, and nodded.

Mim continued, "Your imp is quite right, bowels emptied everywhere. It was quite . . . unpleasant. At first, Hades had anyone who vomited or soiled themselves clean up the mess, but that only brought on another wave of unfortunate purging.

Eventually, even Hades could see that the afflicted were too sick to work. He ordered them to the river to bathe. He ordered me to release any creature in the dungeon with enough wits and strength to clean the great hall. Hades retreated to his private chambers with a half barrel of wine and three unafflicted nymphs. The cleaning of the great hall took days."

Mim shuddered at the memory and sipped his tea. He continued, "When the great hall was fit for use, Hades held an assembly. He announced that he was bored in his underground palace and saw no reason to tolerate the presence of the duplicitous hateful wench—that's you, young mistress—he'd been forced to marry. Henceforth, when you, Persephone, are in the Underworld, he will reside here on Earth, at his Temple of Elis. When you leave the caves to return to Earth every spring, he will resume his residence in Hell. Then he dismissed the assembly, ordered me to clear away what remained of the three nymphs he'd taken into seclusion, and set out for Elis, where he murdered all the priests at his Temple there. He blamed them for the magic pomegranate."

Demeter slapped her forehead with her palm. "Honestly, Hades is an idiot! Does he think he's the only one who can lie and falsify a maker's mark?! Unbelievable, all of the men in that part of the family, Zeus, Poseidon, Hades! I've met bags of rocks who had more sense than those three put together."

Dap giggled at the goddess' outburst, and Mim shook his head in rueful reflection. "You are not the first to wonder about those three, Great Lady."

Persephone nodded, contemplating. "There's an angle here for Mim. I wonder what it is?" she thought. She took a sip of her own sweet tea, and felt her shoulders relax a little. Dap's small body was warm on her lap, and she stroked his mottled black and red skin. He made the low rasping sound that is the imp's equivalent to a cat's purr. She glanced at her mother. Demeter nodded her encouragement.

"Mim, thank you for telling us all this. Forgive me, but I cannot help but think there is something here you want, beyond letting me know that my dread-husband has vacated the premises."

Mim bowed his head. "Yes, young mistress, there is something I want. But first, please know that I am pledged by magic and by my honour to the Throne of the Underworld. That is unbreakable magic. If Hades is not on the Throne, I do not serve him. When you sit there, I serve you." Mim looked up, bulbous brown eyes pleading.

Persephone bit her lip while she thought and stroked Dap. "I know I am bound by magic to return to Underworld, but nothing in the spell compels me to sit the Throne. Can I simply order you to sit on it?"

Mim sighed. "You could, but me trying to take it will result in my death by lightening." Tears welled in his eyes.

Persephone leaned forward and placed her small warm hand on Mim's forearm. "Oh, Mim, do not cry. I do not mean to order you to murder yourself. I do not have that kind of hate in my heart."

Mim sighed deeply and dabbed at his eyes with his silky hanky. "Thank you. Truly, thank you. I have lived under that threat from Hades for hundreds of years."

Persephone leaned back, nodding. "I see," she said, her mind fitting pieces together.

Demeter caught her daughter's eye. "You are drawing some conclusions, I think?"

"Yes, Mother, I am. The Underworld requires either Hades or me to sit on the Throne to administer all aspects of the dead. No one else can wear that mantle. Mim is compelled by strong magic to carry out the wishes of the Throne, regardless of his better judgement. And under Hades' rule, the Underworld has been a brutal and cruel place. Mim is here because he hopes I am different from Hades, and he thinks I can do better."

"Well said, young mistress," said Mim, nodding his head.

Persephone thought some more, stroking Dap's leathery skin. His gravelly purr grew louder. At last she said, "I can change the Underworld during the months I am there, but Hades, being Hades, will change it back during the next rotation."

Mim nodded. "Yes, that is true. He will also, once he's bored of pouting and drinking and raping and killing his way across the island of Elias, try to murder you."
Persephone and Demeter nodded.

Mim continued. "We can't control that, but we can prepare you for it. The souls in the Underworld have suffered greatly, many for no reason other than Hade's spite and caprice.

They will support you, if only for the six months' of respite and the promise of more to come."

Persephone looked at Demeter. "Mother?"

"It's your choice, dear, but really your only choice. Seize the power, daughter."

Persephone nodded, expression grave. "I understand."

Tears welled in Mim's eyes. He sank to his knees before her, head bent. "Thank you, young Queen, thank you."

Persephone touched Mim's shoulder. "No need to kneel to me, Mim; we are partners, not master and servant." She raised him up, and put her arm around the old imp's shoulders, giving him a gentle, encouraging squeeze.

Dap, now curled around Persephone's neck like a torc, raised his head. "When do we leave?"

Chapter Seven

Mim, Persephone, Demeter, and Dap tried to leave at dawn for the Underworld. But as they were finishing breakfast and the sky lightened, they saw that low grey clouds obscured the arc of Helios' chariot. Cold white flakes fell everywhere. It was too cold for tunics and sandals.

Demeter rummaged through the stores in her cottage, and found enough bits of fur, wool, and felt to cobble together cloaks, thick tunics, and booties for all the travellers. Persephone experimented with her beginner's spellcraft and came up with magic sturdy enough to waterproof their booties. She had noticed that when the flakes touched anything warmer than themselves, they transformed into simple water.

By the time the warm travelling gear was finished, it was time for lunch.

Helios' weak light had already passed its apex when the four—properly clad, protectively shod, and decently fed—finally set out to walk to the Underworld.

"The flakes aren't turning to water anymore, Mother," Persephone said.

Demeter nodded and said, "Watch this." She exhaled heavily through her nose. Frosty mist spiralled around her face. Dap, curled snug around Persephone's neck, huffed out mist and squealed. "This is the best!"

He jumped from his perch into a fluffy pile of white flakes at the roadside. He disappeared as one who has jumped into a lake, then re-surfaced as though shot from a trebuchet.

"C-c-cold but fun!" he shouted, then, smiling, snapped at the still-falling white flakes with his pointed teeth.

Persephone and Demeter giggled, and even serious Mim smiled at the young imp's pleasure. Dap hooted and dove again into the snow.

"Mother, are you the one changing the weather, maybe accidentally?" asked Persephone as she scooped some of the white stuff into a ball. She had her eye trained on where Dap might pop up next.

"No child, I have made the land fallow, but not this," Demeter replied.

"Any theories, Mim?" asked Persephone.

Dap burst through the snow, and Persephone lobbed the snowball at him. She had aimed for his head but hit his tail instead.

"Oooh! Very cold! Do it again!" Dap whooped and dove.

"Young mistress, I think this is likely Zeus' doing."

"Trying to make a spectacle of the fallow season?" snarked Demeter.

"Yes, to try to shame you. And just because he can." The elderly imp shook his head.

"Honestly, what was I thinking lying with that man? I must be an idiot," muttered Demeter.

Persephone scooped up more snow, and readied herself for Dap's next jump.

"Mother, as you have said yourself, what's done is done, and without him, you wouldn't have made me."

The older woman sighed, mist swirling around her head. "Yes, you are right. Pity I laid with him before I had perfected parthenogenesis."

Dap leapt from the snow, and this time Persephone's snowball caught him in the middle of his narrow chest. He gasped with laughter, then leapt into her arms.

She dusted the snow from his clothes, and he exclaimed, "Winter is excellent! I love snow!"

Persephone grinned. "Right?! I could do this all day!"

Mim frowned, looking at the sky. "I wish we could, children, but I can feel the night gathering in Helios' chariot's wake. Furthermore, young mistress, I think your spellcraft on our footwear is starting to wear off." He looked down at his booties. "My feet are distinctly . . . soggy."

Persephone's brow furrowed. "Oh dear. I apologize, Mim. We should hurry, then."

Mim bowed from the shoulders. "No need to apologize, child, spells are rarely perfect in their first draft. It's a clever idea, and you've got the next six months to practice it."

The young goddess nodded. "Do you think Zeus will make it snow every day in winter?"

"Oooh, you think he might?!" piped Dap as he curled his lithe body around Persephone's throat.

Mim pulled his cloak tight around his body, crossing his arms over his chest. "He might, at least until he gets bored. He is constantly inconstant. His pride will not allow your mother to win without paying a price."

Demeter scowled and looked up at the sky. She said, "Fallow land, my doing. Cold and frozen flakes? Fine, we can persevere." She sighed, and her face grew pink with anger. "But shorter days? When we all have so much to do? That's a real dick move, Zeus!"

Mim raised his eyebrows to his hairline. "Madam, forgive me, but let's not tempt our fates. You know how . . . touchy the gentleman in question can be."

Demeter sighed, defeated. "You're right, Mim, you're right." Her shoulders slumped.

"Let us hurry on our way, it is not much farther," Mim suggested.

"Very well. Let's away."

The travellers picked up their pace, but Persephone thought she heard her mother mutter "I still say it's a dick move."

Chapter Eight

When the travellers arrived at the main gates of the Underworld, it was deserted. The snow was not as heavy on the ground here. The skeletal trees were coated in diamond-hard ice that glistened as the moon, a pale chilly disk, rose.

"Where's Cerebos?" asked Demeter, referring to the massive three-headed dog who usually guarded the mouth of Hell.

"Hades took him along when he and his entourage moved to Elis for the winter," said Mim.

"How are we supposed to keep the entrance guarded?" Persephone asked.

Mim cleared his throat. "Since you asked . . . he said, and I quote: 'tell that little bitch it's her problem now'. Then he laughed. Had he possessed mustachios, no doubt he would have twirled them."

The goddess rolled their eyes, and Dap piped, "Why does he have to make everything into winning and losing?"

"It's just how he is," said Mim and Demeter in resigned unison.

Persephone looked from the wizened imp to her mother, then back. Stroking the loose, scaly skin on Dap's neck as he rode her shoulder, she said, "Hades is his own problem, at least for now. Let's forget about him until circumstances force us to think about him."

Demeter opened her mouth as if to object, changed her mind, and said instead, "Well said, daughter. One problem at a time. Any thoughts on security?"

"Yes. As I see it, the main concerns right now, at least until Hades returns from Elis to take his turn on the throne, are the risk of curious humans wandering into the Underworld, dead souls drifting out without authorization, and the spies Hades has certainly left behind for sabotage; anything to add, Mim?" Persephone said.

"Indeed, young mistress, just so," said Mim, adjusting the fuzzy knit cap on his head. He shivered.

"Alright then. Putting first things first, passages to the Underworld. Mother, I have an idea, but not the magic to carry it out. Can you help?"

"Certainly. That's why I'm here."

"Excellent! So what about this: encircle the whole of the Underworld's earthly territory with an enchanted river."

"Interesting. That would take care of this main entrance, the service corridors into the kitchen, and any opening from Hell that spills out onto the earthly plane that we don't know about."

Dap sat up straighter on Persephone's shoulder, alert. "There are lots of those! I used them all the time to avoid getting kicked in crowded hallways. Some of Hades' favourites treated me like a football!"

Persephone stroked Dap's tail where it curled in a graceful spiral against her collarbone. "Poor Dap! I'm sad they used to kick you. No longer, not while I rule."

"I know that," he said and stroked Persephone's plump cheek carefully with the curved side of a talon.

Mim cleared his throat, and glanced down at his wet footwear.

"Oh dear, your feet!" said Persephone, "Is it safe to simply walk in, Mim?"

"In truth, I am not certain, young mistress." He sneezed.

"I've got this," said Demeter. With a wave of her hand, steam rose from Mim's booties as the felt dried. A small finger-wagging and she was covered in a mirrored glamour so she could not be seen. If you looked at her, you saw only your own startled reflection, surrounded by trees and any other background.

Dap squealed. "Ooh, the perfect disguise! Can you teach me?"

"Perhaps," came Demeter's disembodied voice. "But for now, be still and quiet while I investigate."

They knew Demeter had walked toward the mouth of Hell because they could hear her felted boots on the snow.

Ten minutes later, they heard the same soft crunching. Since it had started to snow again during Demeter's brief absence, Persephone could see her mother's footprints appear, one by one, as Demeter walked back from the cave opening.

"Mother?" whispered Persephone.

"Yes, dear, just a moment." A slight movement of the air, and Demeter dropped her mirrored glamour. She looked aggrieved and rumpled. She was holding a handkerchief to her bleeding nose.

"Mother, you are injured!" said Persephone, alarmed.

"It's nothing, just a tussle with a confused witch who did not understand the lawfulness of my presence in Hell. She does now, or at least, she will when she comes to."

"A stunning spell, Madam?"

"A rabbit punch to the throat, a solid shove, and a couple of kicks to the face, actually." Demeter shrugged. "Underworld rules: if she doesn't want something, she shouldn't start something."

The company's eyes grew round, and their eyebrows rose in unison.

Demeter shrugged again. "I'm all for peace, but let's not kid ourselves; no coup is ever entirely bloodless."
Mim sighed and shook his head. "Sad but true, I think."

"Did you find any booby traps?" asked Persephone

"A few, then I realized I was going about it all wrong," Demeter said.

45

"How so?" asked Persephone.

"Better to show you," replied the older goddess.

Demeter pocketed the bloody handkerchief, pressed her palms together, stood up straight, and closed her eyes. A ball, glowing pink as a soap bubble sighted through the rays of rosy dawn, started to form between her palms. As she moved her hands further apart, the bubble grew. She blew on it, gently, and a ripple trilled over the bubble's surface. It grew larger. Within moments Demeter had a shimmering pink translucent bubble some eight feet in diameter resting on the snow beside her.

"Oooh, can I pop it?!" asked Dap, dazzled by the bubble's ever-moving surface. Moonlight pooled and eddied across it, hypnotic.

Demeter placed a warm hand on the small imp's narrow shoulder. She smiled at him. "Dap, you have the heart of a lion, but you could not pop this bubble, even if I were to allow it.'

"Most fascinating, Madam, what's is it constructed from?" asked Mim.

Demeter grinned at him, the lines at the corners of her eyes crinkling. "Magic."

Mim hhrumphed under his breath but said no more.

Demeter held up her left thumb and slowly, a glowing pink bubble formed there. When it was the size of a grape, Demeter said, "This large bubble is our transportation and our protection." Pointing with her chin at her thumb, she continued, "the small bubble is your entry and exit key."

She brushed Dap between his eyebrows with her thumb, and the pink bubble stuck there.

"Go ahead, jump in," she said.

The small imp needed no other encouragement. He leapt from Persephone's shoulder as if propelled by springs. His small body passed through the bubble skin as one dives into a lake. Once inside, he bounced against all of the inner surfaces of the bubble. They could not hear his exclamations, but his broad grin and delighted leaps communicated his glee.

"Madam, must I jump to enter?" asked Mim as Demeter pressed a grape-sized pink bubble from her thumb to Mim's brow.

"Of course not, Mim. How undignified. I would never ask that of you!" Demeter said.

Mim nodded gravely, and merely stepped through the barrier into the bubble.

Left thumb aloft with a third small bubble balanced on it, Demeter brushed her daughter's brow. "Sweet one, you have your choice, enter with dignity or play with your small companion; it's up to you."

Persephone nodded. "Tempting to play, but I am Queen of the Underworld for now, at least until Hades' murders me, so best to practice my decorum."

Demeter set a small pink bubble between her own eyebrows and holding her daughter's hand they entered the bubble together.

Chapter Ten

During the first month of that first winter, Persephone practiced various forms of magic every day, under Demeter's watchful eye. Mim and Dap tended the household and liaised with the few souls and witches Hades had left behind. They set the ones they found trustworthy to work cleaning, repairing, and refurbishing Hell. They also organized and managed a squad of retainers to care for the souls of the newly dead. Human beings on the earthly plane had not stopped dying simply because Hell was under new management. Holding the souls of the newly dead in stasis while they waited for proper processing was a rather larger task than Mim had anticipated because there had been a significant uptick in the newly dead. Many humans had not heeded the warnings about the first winter.

In the second month, Demeter and Persephone worked at enlarging and strengthening the boundaries of their bubble haven. The haven grew larger and more stable every day, expanding chamber by chamber. They would not be able to fill every chamber in Hell with the bubble this year, but over successive winters the magical protection would expand to fill the whole realm.

Near the end of the fifth month, the goddesses had just started to discuss the practicalities of terraforming rivers around Hell when Mim joined them in their private bubble-lined chamber.

"Majesties, a word?" asked the wizened imp, pausing at the threshold of the open door.

Persephone smiled. "Yes, Mim, of course. How can we help?"

"I regret to inform you that we have almost reached capacity in terms of holding the souls of the newly dead."

"Meaning what?" asked Demeter, left eyebrow raised.

Mim licked his lips, and twisted his polka dot handkerchief in his hands. "It means that we must start processing souls unless we are prepared to allow . . . diffusion."

Demeter let out a quiet breath.

Persephone said "What's that?"

Persephone looked from her mother to Mim and then back again, her face a question.

Demeter said, "Every soul belongs somewhere, daughter, either anchored to a corporeal body on the earthly plane, or untethered to flesh but anchored to Hell or other realms."

"Just so, Majesty," said Mim, nodding vigorously. "Because we have no processing ceremony at the moment, Dap, the other imps, and I use our collective magic to hold them here in Hell temporarily."

"Okay . . ." said Persephone, silken brows drawing together.

"But the number of souls we imps can sustain with our magic is proportional to the number of imps available to do the work."

"And you are running out of magic to hold so many souls in stasis?"

"Precisely."

"I don't understand- why do we have so many newly dead souls all of a sudden?" asked Persephone.

Demeter sighed, and shifted in her carved wooden chair. "Because human beings are stupid and many did not heed the warnings provided by witches and oracles."

Persephone thought for a moment. "So many more died in the past few months than is typical?" she asked.

Mim dabbed his shiny forehead with his spotted handkerchief, nodding all the while. His face looked grey and drawn, more wizened than usual.

"Mim, you look unwell, is that a side effect of the soul storage approaching capacity?" asked the young goddess.

Mim nodded again, and said, "Do not worry about me, young mistress. It is a strain, but I shall recover once we can start to process the backlog."

"And this is why Dap has been a bit subdued of late, is it not?"
"Yes, young mistress."

Persephone looked at her mother. "Can't we simply allow this backlog of souls to diffuse?"
Mim winced, and Demeter's eyes flashed.

Demeter calmed herself, then spoke. "No, daughter, we should not allow diffusion; it is the final death for that being."

Persephone asked, "What does that mean?"

Demeter's face settled into grim lines, her beauty momentarily diminished. She looked haggard and tired, Persephone thought.

Demeter explained, "As long as a soul is anchored to a corporeal body or to one of the etheric realms, such as Hades, Tartarus, Elysium or a few other places, consciousness continues. The soul is aware of itself, in other words."

"All right," Persephone nodded.

"When souls diffuse, they . . . break apart into tiny pieces. The tiny pieces drift further and further apart and are absorbed into the fabric of the Universe. When the particles get far enough apart, consciousness snuffs out, like this."

Demeter leaned forward and pinched the wick-tip of one of the lit candles on the worktable. The light was gone; smoke drifted lazily up toward the ceiling of the chamber.

Persephone's eyes grew round, her mouth a perfect "O".

Mim cleared his throat. "Hades would threaten many souls who served him with diffusion when he was displeased. And sometimes, he would allow the newly dead to diffuse in front of his entire court. He thought it was a form of . . . entertainment." Mim hung his head and stared at his feet.

Tears welled in Persephone's eyes. She placed her hand on Mim's forearm and gently squeezed.

Voice shaking with righteousness, Persephone said, "Mim, we aren't going to allow that. I am so sorry about what you had to endure under Hades' rule."

The old imp kept his head bowed, dabbing at his eyes with his silken handkerchief.

Demeter sighed. "I had hoped that we would have had more time to work on infrastructure, but you are quite right, daughter; we cannot weaken the imps or allow wholesale soul-diffusion." The elder goddess pressed her lips together, giving her face a stern cast.

"Mother," asked Persephone, "Do you think that Hades knew we would be inundated with the souls of the newly dead?"

"Oh, more than that, I am sure. He likely found a way to counter our warnings about winter. Probably thousands have died that would not have, had he not interfered. Never forget, darling daughter, he wants your rule to be disastrous. Killing off a large number of humans is part of that."

Persephone's face went pale. "But if so many humans die, and the survivors then refuse to sacrifice to the gods, Zeus may remove you from the pantheon, replace you."

"Worse than that, daughter. I think Hades' larger plan is to convince Zeus to press the re-set button on the whole planet."

"So he would not only kill some of the pantheon of gods—you, Hecate, me, maybe Artemis—but also wipe out the entire human race and start again?"

The older goddess nodded, lips a grim line. "I think that's exactly what he plans to do."

Persephone's face flushed pink. "All because of a partial defeat here in Hell? Ugh! Mother, I . . . I . . . hate him. I truly do!"

Demeter stood up and placed a steadying hand on Persephone's shoulder. "We all do, dear one, we all do."

Chapter Eleven

The goddesses set aside their river-making plans, and with Mim's advice, started work on processing souls.

Everything they tried failed.

The souls, regardless of how willing they were, would simply not bind to the Underworld or anywhere else. Weeks of effort yielded nothing but frustration and tears.

They were a mere week away from the end of their last month in Hell when Mim had an insight while pouring over some old books for the tenth time.

The wrinkled imp rushed to the goddess's work room, a massive old book under his arm.

"I think I have it, majesties!" he explained, panting and out of breath from his exertion.

Demeter looked up from the map she was perusing, and Persephone stopped pacing. Dap rode her shoulder, awake and flicking the tip of his tail.

Persephone said, "What is it? We have almost no time left."

Demeter said nothing. She had started to give up hope.

Mim placed the book on the table, and started to page through it. His talons scratched the pages of parchment as he flipped pages.

"Here it is," he said. "Majesties, please have a look at this."

Persephone and Demeter stood on either side of the imp, looking to where he pointed.

"'Every master in Hell must find his own way'. What is that supposed to mean?" Persephone asked, not daring to hope.

Mim mopped his moist brow with his handkerchief. "I take it to mean that anyone with the magical authority over the Underworld can craft administrative or operational spells for the Underworld."

Persephone's eyes grew round. "We can make whatever we want?"

Mim took a seat at the table. "Not quite as simple as that." He licked the tip of a talon and with great care used it to turn the parchment pages of the ancient, crumbling book. "The power to make your way extends just to the boundaries of the Underworld and no further."

Demeter nodded. "That makes sense," she said. "Extending your powers past the boundaries of the Underworld will surely draw the attention of Zeus and maybe a few other gods."

"Right, and we don't want that," Persephone added. She stroked the scales on Dap's tail as it lay curled against her collarbone. "How big a magical working can it be?"

"What do you mean by "big," young Mistress?" asked Mim.

Persephone took a seat at the table beside Mim. "What I'm wondering is this: can I change some of the fundamental workings of the Underworld, provided there is no impact on realms under the magical authority of others?"

Mim raised a brow, and turned another crumbling page. "Based on what I've read here, young mistress, yes, you can."

"What do you have in mind, daughter?"

"Well, it's clear we need to find a way to process all of the dead before they disincorporate. There's no point in trying all the things we've tried already. All those magics were leftover from Hades' reign. We're not Hades, and it's pointless to try to use his magics. We need to make something new."

"How so?" asked Demeter.

"Let me put it this way: the status quo since the rise of the Pantheon has been that Hades ruled the Underworld. He put in minimal magic, just enough to process souls to a minimum of effectiveness. But his main pursuits have always been centred on his own pleasures. He was simply too lazy to plan or organize the incoming souls. As a result, until now, souls have drifted where they want. There's no focus or organization."

Mim cocked his head at Persephone, expectant.

"So what if we did a magical working around the edges of the Underworld such that every soul that crosses into the Underworld must undergo examination and judgement?"

"And then what, daughter?"

57

"Then they are assigned a place to go—Hades, Tartarus, Elysium et cetera—based on that judgement."

"Your majesty, who will sit in judgement?" asked Mim.

"I will."

"Not to offend, young mistress, but allow me to argue the other side. Why should you get to judge them?"

"Because I am Queen of the Underworld and fixing the Underworld is my job."

Mim smiled. "As good an answer as any other, young mistress."

They drew their chairs closer to the table and started to plan.

Chapter Twelve

Once Persephone had perfected the judgement process magically, it was a simple thing to add some theatrics to the ceremony- a golden scale, a polished ebony headpiece with horns, a jewelled sceptre for pointing and gesturing. None of these props were essential, but they helped the souls stay focused, which made assessment and judgment work more smoothly.

After a couple of false starts, the goddesses worked out a system. Once a day, Demeter would traverse the Underworld, gathering any newly arrived souls to her bosom. She led them to Persephone right away, as the newly arrived were easier to process than souls that had been held in stasis for months by imp magick. The rest of the time, Demeter retrieved souls from stasis and brought them, bleary-eyed and blinking, to her daughter. Persephone sat on her throne in her judgement day costume, looking—she hoped—fierce and formidable. She reviewed the life of each soul and determined their proper placement in the magickal realms. Then she bound them to their proper places with a spell.

The only problem was the sheer volume of accumulated souls. Neither goddess was sure they would be able to process them all before their time in the Underworld was over and they had to return to Earth.

Persephone did not mind the long hours of routine, uncreative magic. It is easy to work hard at something simple. She found it relaxing—meditative, even.

Not so Demeter, who grew bored and restless easily. She preferred to start things, not finish them. But to her credit, she never stopped helping Persephone conduct the judgement ceremony.

The goddesses and imps worked eighteen-hour days, stopping for only brief periods to nap or take some bread and wine. Dap and Mim made sure the goddesses were supported with cups of tea and shoulder massages.

At moonrise on their last night in the Underworld, Mim calculated they had only a couple of hundred souls left to judge.

"Oh dear, I'm not sure we're going to make it," said Persephone when Mim informed her of the numbers. "We've been averaging thirty souls processed per work hour . . ."

"Which means we could probably get ninety more processed by midnight," said Demeter.

Dap, lying curled up on a velvet cushion near Persephone's feet, sat up. Alarm was writ in his every muscle, his every twitch.

Dap said, "Which means what, that Hades will allow the one hundred-and-some others to simply snuff out into nothingness?"

Persephone sighed, tears welling into her eyes. Voice soft, she said, "Yes, it might mean that."

Demeter opened her mouth to reply, but before she could, a voice rang out in the hallway just outside the goddess' work room.

"It most definitely means that," boomed Hades, standing just at the threshold of the work room.

"How did you get in here, Hades? The realm does not change hands until the witching hour. We still have a few hours left," said Demeter.

Hades scoffed and gulped some wine from the jewelled goblet in his hand. "Not enough time to finish the task. Neither of you has the power I have." His teeth, stained grey from the wine, made his grin macabre.

Demeter chuckled. "Pretty to think so, I'm sure. If you have so much power Hades, why not cross the threshold into our chamber? I think you cannot."

Hades smirked. "I think I can."

He attempted a step forward. There was a sizzle and the smell of ozone, but he could not complete the motion. Sparks travelled over his armour.

"Is that the best you can do, woman? That spell is a mere tickle!"

Now it was Demeter's turn to smile. "An effective tickle, it would seem."

Hades scowled and quaffed more wine.

"Tell me, kind husband, was it always your plan to have so many humans die, even unto dying the final death?" asked Persephone, a tremor in her voice.

"Of course, you witless girl. I grow weary of your mother's interference and your defiance. Better if Zeus starts again. Who cares how many humans die? Doesn't matter to me. And we've replaced uncooperative goddesses before, and each time, Zeus crafts a world more to my liking."

"How can you be so cruel? What has brought you to this?" Persephone exclaimed.

"Just made that way, sweetling. We all have our qualities," Hades said.

Demeter walked toward the chamber entrance. "We do indeed have our qualities," she announced, "and one of yours is 'locked out of this room.'" She slammed the heavy door in Hades' face.

Unable to penetrate the protective bubble, he cursed and banged on the chamber door. "You bitches have just three more hours, and then Hell is mine again! Don't think this silly bubble spell will keep me out that long, either!"

"Ignore him," said Demeter.

Mim's greyish skin paled. "I'm not sure we'll be able to bring more souls in here with him lurking in the hallway. Majesties, maybe now is the time to leave the Underworld. There is nothing we can do for the unprocessed souls now."
Demeter frowned but said nothing.

Dap started to wail.

"No," said Persephone.

Demeter, Dap, and Mim looked at her in surprise.

"I said 'no.' No leaving early, no sacrificing over two hundred souls, no triggering Zeus hitting the reset button on the gods and human race. No. There is another way."

Mim cleared his throat. "With respect, majesty, what way is that?"

"I don't know yet, but I will find one."

Chapter Thirteen

Persephone said, "Is he still out there?"

Standing on a chair pulled up to the door, Dap peered through the keyhole.

"The hallway is clear," he said.

"Right," said Persephone, "Time for the throne room and the big finish."

She surveyed the wreckage in the work room. Calibration issues during the last hours of magickal practice had taken a toll: small water spills had become indoor ponds, their edges fringed with rapidly-growing moss and speckled red cap mushrooms. Even the pink silk tapestry on the wall had not escaped unscathed; one drooping corner trailed into a muddy puddle.

Persephone sighed and stretched. "It's a mess in here now," said the young goddess, "but if this works, that won't matter." It won't matter if this doesn't work, either, but no sense pointing that out. It will just upset Dap.

Persephone adjusted her horned headdress, and twitched the velvet skirts of her dress, black as ink. She picked up her golden sceptre and brass scales from the worktable. While made of rich fabric, Persephone's dress was unornamented, severe. She hoped that with the headdress on, she looked formidable.

"It's now or never, Dap. Time to meet up with Mother and Mim in the throne room. Can you get my train?" she asked.

"Yes, mistress," said Dap as he leapt off the chair. He pushed the chair off to one side, out of the way of the door, and scrambled behind Persephone, gripping the fine fabric of Persephone's train.

"Don't forget our bubbles!" reminded Dap.

"Not to worry, I've got them right here," said Persephone as she drew two small shining pink spheres from her pocket. Light played over the surface of each bubble as if they were made of soap. Persephone pressed one to her forehead, between the eyebrows, then turning and bending, did the same for Dap. The protective pink magic that surrounded the work room and barred entry to Hades or anyone else with evil intentions would now move with them as they walked through the corridors to the throne room.

Young woman and imp walked slowly through the corridors. Haste would imply uncertainty, nervousness, weakness. Persephone knew that Hades' spies could be virtually anywhere, and she knew tales of her rushing in panic through the corridors would entertain him. *I think he's had more than enough entertainment.* She forced herself to relax her tight shoulders as she walked.

The throne room was ablaze in light. Everyone in the Underworld had turned up for the exchange of power from Persephone to Hades. Hades was there, to the left of the great carved throne, along with his entourage of lickspittles, miscreants, and flunkies. They jeered when Persephone crossed the threshold. Persephone's retainers filled the rest of the room, anxiety clearly writ on every face. No one knew what Hades might do when he regained control of the Underworld.

Demeter and Mim stood before the throne, working together to keep a densely packed collection of souls in one place. They both bore a protective pink bubble on their brows.

"Mother," called Persephone over the sniggers of Hades' followers.

"Yes, daughter?"

"I am ready to begin."

"As am I," said Demeter, bowing her head. The bubble of pink magic that Demeter had worn just over her skin started to expand. Mim's bubble also started to expand, the two bubbles joining into one large one. Even from half a hall away, Persephone could hear her mother's steady breathing as the older goddess's breath grew the pink bubble. In moments it was large enough to encase everyone in the hall except Hades, his minions, and the collected souls.

"Ha!" shouted Hades. "Do you see this? They are not even trying to deal with the remaining souls. They are running away like scared children!"

"We're not running anywhere," said Persephone, voice calm and low.

The great hall shook momentarily, dust and few pebbles falling from the ceiling. Then the throne room was still and quiet. A moment passed, then another. Hades opened his mouth to jeer again, but before he could make a sound, a rivulet of flowing earth burst from underneath the great hall floor.

Hades and his pets stared at it.

Persephone moved her sceptre slightly to the right, and the flowing trail of earth formed first one bank, then the other. The two banks of earth ran in parallel from the middle of the throne room to the double-doored entrance and beyond.

With a flick of Persephone's wrist, wild grasses and delicate moss covered the banks. A spring fountained up from the center of the throne room floor, water filling the space between the banks.

Persephone caught her mother's eye and nodded. Demeter nodded back and clapped her hands.

A small wooden boat appeared, half drawn onto the bank closest to the throne.

"What are you two up to?" shouted Hades.

"You'll see," Demeter muttered to herself.

"Mim, the volunteer?" asked Persephone.

"Yes, young majesty, right here," said the elderly imp. He used a gentle controlled talon to pick a single wispy soul from the corralled group.

It floated toward Persephone. She held out her hand, and the misty soul wrapped itself around her left forearm.

Persephone looked at the soul on her arm.

"You are ready and willing to serve me?" she asked.

The soul glowed as though lit from within.

"And you agree to one hundred years of service before you are sent onward?"

The soul glowed again.

"It shall be so," she said, her voice loud and firm.

She made a stirring motion with her left hand. Misty soul-stuff dropped to the floor, lit from within by a thousand suns.

When the light dimmed, the wispy soul was gone, and in its place stood a hooded figure, holding a pole.

"I name you Charon the ferryman, and I name this river Styx," said Persephone. The crowd in the throne room murmured. Truth be told, the so-called river was more a stream than a river, but it would serve.

"Why are you ruining a perfectly good throne room by having a river run through it, you stupid girl!" shouted Hades.

Persephone looked over in Hades' direction and said, "You'll see."
Her visage was grim, and Hades could swear that he saw flames burning in Persephone's eyes. A trick of the light, perhaps.

Persephone stepped to where her mother and Mim were maintaining some newly-out-of-stasis souls in a rough grouping.

"It's time," she said.

Persephone held both her hand above her head as she said, "Come to me, souls."

The densely packed souls started to swirl as they started to glow from within. One by one, the wisps wrapped themselves around Persephone's hands and forearms, by necessity becoming denser as they did so. When all the souls were wrapped around her hands and forearms, Persephone brought her hands together and murmured a wordless spell. The souls compacted themselves into a dense ball no larger than a pomegranate. It fit perfectly in Persephone's hand and had a pleasing springy density.

"Denizens of the Underworld," said Persephone, looking at the remaining souls and other entities in the throne room. "Today, I usher a new era."

The crowd started to whisper.

"Here I have souls who risk disincorporation. I will stand in judgement of them and decide their fate," she continued.

She knelt on the floor, oblivious of her dress's fine fabric and the small bits of earth that had managed to escape from the magickal terraforming of the River Styx.

"Every master in Hell must make his own way, I am told. Here is my way. Every soul will be weighed and judged. Then those souls will be assigned to their proper realm."

She placed the dense ball of souls on one of the plates that depended from the crossbar of the brass scales.

"This group of souls will . . ."

"What did you say? You're weighing them all together? You can't do it that way!" shouted Hades, eyebrows lifted to his hairline.

Persephone's eyes flicked briefly to him. "I have found my way, Hades."

The pink bubble around her sizzled. *Hades' magic. He's trying to stop me.* Ignoring him, she removed a pomegranate from her pocket. She placed it on the other scale plate. Persephone passed her left hand over the brass scales, careful not to touch any part of the scales themselves.

"I weigh the kindness and generosity of these souls against this pomegranate. If these souls weigh less than a pomegranate, I will give them to Charon to take to Tartarus; if more, Charon will take them to the Elysian Fields," Persephone said.

Hades said, "You can't weigh them as a group . . . that's not . . . fair. I order you to . . ."

"Be quiet," said Persephone, eyes flashing.

The crowd was silent. Persephone held her breath and watched the scale tip from side to side. The sides of the scale paused a moment in perfect equipoise. *I wonder which way it will go.* The plate holding the soul-ball sank to the floor.

Everyone in the crowd, excepting Hades' minions, cheered.

Persephone announced, "And with that, Hades, we will leave you to rule for the next six months as agreed."

Dap handed Persephone the dense ball of souls. Persephone turned the rubbery sphere over in her hand. She gave the ball to Charon, who pocketed it. Persephone whispered something to Charon, who climbed into his boat. He started to pole himself along the stream the young goddess had terraformed, away from the throne room. A few of those who serve in the Underworld—curious about the end result of Persephone's handiwork—trotted alongside him on the riverbank, intent on following him to Elysian Fields.

Persephone swept from the room, Dap holding her train. Mim and Demeter followed, leaving Hades grumbling to his lickspittles, miscreants, and flunkies. Persephone's heart pounded in her chest all the way back to the workroom, but no one, not even her mother, could see her fear.

"Daughter, that was well done. I confess I am surprised he gave up that easily," Demeter remarked.
"He's given up just for now. I think the terraforming and aggregate soul-weighing were not things he was expecting. As soon as he can, he will try to ruin or disrupt that spellwork," said Persephone.

Dap sighed in aggravation. "He'll never give up trying to mess with us, will he?" he asked, not expecting an answer.

Slumped in a chair in the workroom, Demeter idly waved her fingers in the air, urging the items she wanted to take back to her cottage into packing themselves into a rucksack. Persephone tried to bring some order to the massive piles of books that littered the table. Dap sorted bottles of essential oils into 'staying' and 'going' piles.

Within the hour the goddesses, along with Dap, had departed from the Underworld. The women walked through the thawing landscape back to Demeter's cottage while Dap rode on Persephone's shoulder. Even though Spring had arrived, the three could still see their breath, though snow and ice had already started to melt away. The moon was crisp-edged with cold and the lonely stars shivered. They walked in silence.

The three had a tacit arrangement to avoid discussing Mim and the fact his magical bond to the Underworld would keep him at Hades' side for the next six months. They also refrained from speculating how Hades might kill or torment Mim for daring to serve Persephone when it was her turn to rule. One problem at a time thought Persephone as she walked through the cold mud.

They reached the cottage in the hours just before dawn. All three fell into an exhausted sleep and slept solidly until noon. They awoke to the smell of coffee and bacon. Dap wandered into the kitchen, rubbing his bulbous eyes, to find that the goddesses had beaten him to it. Persephone sat in front of an enormous pile of pancakes, Demeter sipped coffee in silent bliss, and Mim—wearing a frilly white cotton eyelet apron—was presiding over a pan of hissing, spattering bacon.

"Mim!" shouted Dap. He ran to the rounder, larger imp and hugged him. "What are you doing here? How did you convince Hades to let you go?" The tip of the young imp's tail twitched in curiosity.

"Let me finish cooking breakfast, and I shall tell the tale," said Mim. He removed Dap's arms from around his middle, and poured a half cup of coffee for Dap, topping it up the rest of the way with milk.

Mim was as good as his word, so as soon as the bacon was finished cooking and had been distributed alongside the pancakes, he started to talk:

"When you all left the throne room, I knew I should not follow. I had one of Demeter's pink bubbles in my pocket, so I knew if it came to some kind of confrontation between Hades and me, I could blow the bubble into a suit to offer myself some protection from his wrath. If I could inflate the bubble in time."

"Hades, of course, was shocked by the appearance of the river Styx in the throne room, and all that you did with the souls, young mistress." Mim nodded at Persephone. Syrup on her chin, she nodded back. Mim cleared his throat and sipped his tea.

"And he was quite preoccupied with the unexpected arrival of Zeus. Hades spent at least half an hour trying to convince Zeus to smite all of you for your impudence, but Zeus seemed entertained by it all—the terraforming, the soul weighing, sliding Hades' victory out from under him."

"Partial victory, dear Mim, as that monster is still married to my darling girl, and she is still bound to Hell for six months of the year," said Demeter, then took a sip of her coffee.

"Yes, madam, but you did manage to stave off the end of the world and live again to fight another day."
Demeter frowned and forked a small piece of pancake into her mouth. She nodded.

"So after a couple of hours passed, and his initial shock and confusion wore off, he finally had time to speak with me."

"I bet Hades had terrible things to say," sniffed Dap as he poked at a piece of over-crisp black bacon.

"He did. And he also wanted to know if I had missed serving him, if I'd missed Hell as he had made it, missed our work together in running Hell. Forgive me, majesties, I felt I could do nothing but lie and tell him how overjoyed I was at his return and the fact that the Underworld would be 'going back to normal' now that he's back." Mim dropped his gaze, two bright red circles of shame burning on his cheeks.

Persephone put her soft hand over Mim's taloned one. "There is nothing to be ashamed of Mim, and you did what you had to do to survive. I am glad you did."

Mim paused for a moment, dabbing his eyes with his polka dot handkerchief. He sighed.

"It turns out that I'm glad of it, too. When Hades heard my lies, he believed them. I don't think he can imagine a world where he is not the center of it, so to him it seems reasonable that I want to be in his household and serve him. He loves himself so over-much he cannot imagine others not loving him."

Demeter chuckled. "Well said, Mim."

"Thank you, madam. So when Hades' believed that I wanted nothing more than to continue to serve him as I have done over the years, of course he banished me."

"BANISHED YOU! He banished you?" Persephone said, outraged. "Banishment is the worst punishment, akin to death, how dare he, after all your loyal service . . ."

Demeter put a calming hand on Persephone's forearm. The young goddess remembered herself, and said: "Sorry to interrupt, Mim, please continue."

"He snapped a chunk of wood off the Underworld throne and gave it to me. He said that as long as I kept it with me, my magical obligations to the throne were met, that his only order to me for the next six months was to keep the relic of the throne with me and be out of his sight. I did not deserve the privilege of living with him in Hell. Then he gave me ten minutes to take what I needed of my possessions and get out. Of course I pretended to be distraught, and carried on with wailing, gnashing of teeth. I even rent my clothes a little," he said, gesturing to a small tear in the lapel of his vest.

Demeter laughed. "Well played, Mim. I am very relieved. I had feared the worst might have happened to you before we could figure out a way to free you."

"Yes, it was not what I expected, madam, and I'm tremendously pleased."

A thought suddenly occurred to Demeter, writ plain on her face. "The piece of wood from the throne, do you think he's using it to maybe listen to us?"

"Oh most assuredly, madam," said Mim, smiling broadly.

Persephone, alarmed, said, "Well, we need to do something about that!"

"Already done, young mistress," said Mim, holding up a chunk of polished ebony wood that was completely wrapped in heavy fragrant beeswax.

"It will still let him track me, no doubt, but I do not believe there is a way for him to hear through the wax, maybe just a word or two here and there, enough to think that his spell is faulty, not enough to give him information," said Mim, helping himself to the last pancake.

"Hmm, and do you need to keep it on your person?" asked Demeter.

"Yes, in a pocket or worn around the neck, I think."

Demeter raised a brow. "Would floating behind you in a bubble be close enough?"

"Yes, madam, I think so."

"Let me see what can be done about that for you after breakfast, Mim."

Mim nodded his assent. Demeter and Mim leaned their chairs back against the kitchen walls and made small talk while Dap and Persephone washed the breakfast dishes. The early spring sunshine, weaker in the morning, now streamed through the windows. The light seemed to be growing stronger with every moment.

Black as Coal, Red as Blood

Black as Coal, Red as Blood

On a cold, wet night, an old beggar-woman appeared at my door.

"Give me bread, and let me sit by your fire, and I will tell you a wondrous tale."

I let her in and gave her bread with butter. This is what she said:

She had hair as black as coal; her lips as red as blood; her skin snow-white.

She was a monster. That's why her stepmother tried to kill her. But that jumps ahead in the tale; let's start at the beginning. In the beginning, Drusilla was just a silly princess, playing at magic, not serious about . . . well, not serious about anything, really.

Her parents wanted her to marry the widowed king of a neighbouring land. Drusilla did as she was bid. On the day of her marriage, she thought herself lucky. Her husband had no sons with his dead wife, just a scrawny baby girl who had been born with a caul. Drucilla was certain the babe would not live out the year, and the children of her own body would have the throne in due time.

She was wrong.

That sickly babe grew into a robust child, albeit a trifle pale of cheek. Meanwhile, her own womb shrivelled. Every year she would present the king with yet another stillborn son. Ten stillbirths in ten years. It killed any love he might have had for her. When he died, they were little better than hostile strangers.

Gloriana, his daughter, did not grieve his death as a daughter should. She was almost eleven when it happened, old enough to understand her father was gone forever. The fact she was unaffected by his passing was the first concrete thing Drusilla could point to and say, 'this child is unnatural.' But then, no one listened to her. No one listened until it was far too late. Some even thought Drusilla was trying to steal the crown for herself instead of accepting her role as regent. But Drusilla didn't care who ruled; she wanted to weep over the family that could have been. Gloriana could have the crown and her queenship when she was ready. Drusilla cared naught for all that. She left the ruling to the bureaucrats.

The bureaucrats could see that Drusilla was disinclined to give any mothering to Gloriana. They arranged for the girl to be fostered by a noble family who lived on the other side of the great forest.

Much to the bureaucrats' relief, Drusilla was in no hurry to marry again. Instead, she took the castle huntsman as her lover and turned back to the lessons of magic her mother had tried to impress on her during her youth. Drusilla's mother came from a long line of women with the Sight, able to look through mirrors and bowls of water to view people and places at great remove. Drusilla, too, had this gift, but she was unpracticed. Drusilla wrote to her mother and had her send a silvered looking-glass. She practiced night and day, rarely leaving her chamber, never permitting anyone but the huntsman to enter.

And so it went for five years. Drusilla was immersed in study. Gloriana was with her foster family. And things seemed to find their own rhythms. Gloriana did not write home. Drusilla was glad of that. Drusilla was almost content, almost happy.

After five years, the family of nobles sent Gloriana back. The letter that arrived before the girl did refused to say why. Whatever the circumstances, Gloriana was clearly leaving their home under a cloud of shame and reprobation.

When the girl arrived, Drusilla learned why. Gloriana's feet had transformed. She had dainty cunning black hooves where normal feet should be. Her hooves rang against the flagstone castle floors—clippity clop clippity clop clippity clop. Drusilla was shocked: everyone knew such partial transformations were a mark of something sinister.

Gloriana had only been home for a few days when bodies of men started to turn up in nooks and crannies of the castle with all the blood drained from them.

Drusilla suspected Gloriana at once and told the bureaucrats as much. They pooh-poohed Drusilla and did not take her suspicions seriously. They were so certain that Princess Gloriana was not responsible that Drusilla started to doubt her instincts.

She doubted herself until the night she found Gloriana with her teeth in the neck of the man who guarded Drusilla's chamber. The man was slumped against the wall, eyes rolled back in his head, his lips white. When Gloriana's eyes met Drusilla's, they glowed red like embers in a late evening fire.

Drusilla barred her door against the monstrous girl and woke the huntsman who slumbered in her bed.

She told him what she had seen. She bade him take Gloriana to the forest and kill her. The huntsman agreed. But Gloriana had fled and could not be found.

There were rumours she had been taken in by a family of dwarves, deep in the forest. The mutilated bodies of men started to turn up in the town and the surrounding area. At first, it was men no one would miss—the village drunkard, wife beaters, itinerant mercenaries. After that, it was only one per month, then three, then five. Soon, no miscreants were left to kill, and even men of good reputation were found drained of their blood and with their chests ripped open. She ate the hearts now; the blood alone could not satisfy her.

The bureaucrats were beside themselves. They announced to the kingdom that there was a bounty available if only someone would kill Gloriana and bring back her heart and hooves as proof.

Drusilla scried what she could, but her Sight was limited. She could only ever see Gloriana imperfectly, as though looking at her through pondwater. Gloriana was protected by magics so ancient that they counteracted Drusilla's gift.

But the dwarves who did Gloriana's bidding were not so protected. By finding and following them with the Sight, Drusilla was finally able to see the cave where they lived. She resolved to kill Gloriana through subterfuge.

Drusilla bade the castle cook make some apple tarts. When they were cool, Drusilla poured poison over the tarts and packed them up in a basket. She dressed herself in the rags of an old beggar woman, rubbing dirt on her face and hands. Drusilla cast a glamour on herself, so she appeared old and frail. She took the basket of tarts into the forest as though she was going to leave an offering for Gloriana.

The disguise fooled Gloriana. She accepted the apple tarts as her due. She ate one, then another, then a third. Her hunger knew no bounds. Drusilla watched the demon girl gorge herself on tarts until Gloriana collapsed to the ground, frothing at the mouth from the arsenic.

Certain that her work was complete, Drusilla did not bother to scry what happened to the body. She simply walked away. She did not see the dwarves gather around Gloriana and weep over her; did not see them build her a glass coffin; did not see them lay Gloriana's body to rest inside it bestrewn with flowers and rosy red apples; did not see that Gloriana's body failed to rot and moulder.

The old woman paused in her tale to shove half a slice of bread with butter into her mouth.

Mouth still full she said, "If Drusilla had seen these things, would she have sent the huntsman to cut off the girl's head? Perhaps. Even so, some things can live without their heads. You can never be certain of death unless the body has been given to the fire . . . but that is another story altogether. I want to finish this one."

I spread the last of my butter on the remaining heel of bread and handed it to the old woman. Her tale continued:

The meadow where the dwarves had placed Gloriana's glass coffin got a great deal of direct sunshine. What no one saw was that the body under glass was sweating. As the days warmed and grew longer, the body continued to sweat, moisture condensing on the inside of the glass. The dwarves noted the moisture whenever they came by the coffin to weep and gnash their teeth at Gloriana's demise. They did not know that day by day, drop by drop,

Gloriana was sweating out the poison that had felled her.

On the longest day of the year, under a brilliant sun, a young nobleman passed by the glass coffin with his retinue. He had never seen such a sight before and was fascinated with the beautiful girl kept under glass. He dismounted his horse to investigate. He drew as close as he could. Nestled in dried roses and desiccated apples, she was incomparably lovely. She had hair as black as coal, lips as red as blood, and skin as white as snow. Palm pressed to the glass, he longed to touch the hand resting just inches from his.

When her eyes opened, they glowed like the red embers of a midnight fire. The lordling was overcome by desire and shattered the glass coffin to free her.

She told him, "My wicked stepmother has stolen my crown. Will you help me take it back?"

The young lord agreed. They developed a plan.

On the eve of Lughnasadh, Drusilla took a break from her late-night studies to go in search of some bread and cheese. The witching hour approached, and she was famished. The huntsman was already asleep and snoring, having drunk his fill of ale hours before.

As she wandered the halls of the castle on her way to the kitchen, she called out, "Hello, hello, is anyone there?" But she found no one.

No one living, that is. The first corpse was a surprise. Drusilla's heart pounded inside the cage of her chest. Her hands shook. Her mouth was dry and she wanted to run, run back to her chamber, run from the castle itself.

She had seen Gloriana die. It couldn't be her; it couldn't be. But in her heart, she knew whose work this was.

Drusilla felt drawn to the throne room, whether by magic or fearful compulsion, who can say? She could hear low murmuring. She crept close to the door so she could place her ear on it. But before Drusilla could make out what was being said, she was seized from behind by small strong hands, a pair on each of her arms. She swivelled her head from side to side to look at who had captured her. It was two dwarves.

She tried to wrench herself away from them. They were surprisingly strong; no matter how she thrashed, they would not let go. As she continued to struggle, one of them punched her in the stomach. The blow was hard and left her winded and gasping from the pain. She ceased to struggle. They dragged her into the throne room.

She was almost winded again by what she saw. Human entrails were swagged between the pillars like macabre bunting. A man's body was laid out on a trestle table, the chest open. Gloriana sat crossways on the throne, her long legs dangling over the arm. Her young lordling stood by her side, sneering. Candlelight gleamed off Gloriana's highly polished hooves. She was gnawing on an apple. When she saw Drusilla, a cruel smile spread across her face.

Iron shoes fashioned to look like hooves had already been heated over a fire, and they were brought over to Drusilla with tongs. She had to put on the red-hot hooves and dance until she fell down dead. Gloriana and her lordling consigned Drusilla's body to fire the next day in the town square, right after they announced Gloriana's rule. There were no objectors.

A month later, Gloriana married her young lordling. Together they ruled the kingdom in fire and blood for one hundred years.

The old woman paused and took a bite of her bread and butter.

"That's your tale," she said, her mouth full.

"That's it? That's the end?" I said.
"Yes, that is the end," replied the old woman, firelight flickering over her face. The way the shadows fell made her look hundreds of years old, far older than she could possibly be.

"Surely there is more to tell, good mother. Have some more bread and some of this soup, and when you are refreshed you can tell me the rest."

"You are not a young man, so you have no excuse for being stupid. The end is the end, and that's that."

I sighed. "But it's so grim."

The old woman cackled and spooned some soup into her mostly snaggletoothed mouth.

I watched her eat in silence and listened to the crackling of the fire.

"This was not a fair trade," I thought, resentment swelling in my breast, "the least she could do is give her tale a happy ending. She is cheating me."

She slurped the last of her soup and stuffed the remaining heel of the bread into her mouth, then chewed vigorously. She gave me an appraising look.

"Be careful, for I have been kind so far; very kind, by my reckoning. Now that my meal is through, let me warm my feet by the fire, and then I will be on my way."

I considered arguing with her because I wanted to know how did the townspeople fare, how many of them did Gloriana eat in her one hundred years as sovereign, what became of the wicked Gloriana after her hundred-year rule, but my questions died on my tongue when I noticed the old woman's feet. She had them propped up on the fire's grate. They were not human feet. They were dainty cunning little hooves.

I couldn't stop staring, even when I noticed her watching me do it.

"I think you take my meaning now, don't you?"

"Yes, good mother, I do," I said.

The old woman said, "And since you have been—mostly—a gracious host, I will leave you now in peace."

She stood up, wrapped her cloak tightly around her bent old body, and left my shack.

I spent the rest of that sleepless night huddled by my fire, thinking every rattle of a dry leaf heralded her return. In the morning, I packed a rucksack with as many necessaries as I could reasonably carry and struck off across the fields. If the old woman returned, I did not want to be there to greet her.

I've been walking ever since.

The Singing Harp

The Singing Harp

Chapter One

A thousand leagues from here, in times long past, a woman lived near the north seashore, in Ulster, close to the place the river Bann meets the ocean. In her eighteenth year, she married John the miller.

The year after that she bore three daughters—triplets—as unalike as could be. Though the babes had shared a womb, they did not share a birthday, so long did their mother labour with them.

The eldest of the three was born at noon on April first. Her mother named her Etain, 'beauty so great it inspires jealousy', for this infant was beautiful. Many newborn babes have pinched red faces and pointy heads, but Etain was as lovely as any gilly-flower. She had fair skin touched with pink, rose petal lips, hair as golden as the sun, and eyes as blue as a cloudless summer sky.

The middle sister arrived just a few minutes after midnight on April second. She was born screaming. The midwife made crosses from wild broom, placing them everywhere around the birthing room. She knew, as everyone does, that babes born in the witching hour need extra spiritual protection, especially if they are ugly.

And ugly she was. Not only did the middle sister resemble an angry wrinkled monkey, she was a completely hairless angry wrinkled monkey. The midwife had seen such babes before: in her experience, they usually grew snaggled teeth big as horses', developed pustules on their skin, and stayed bald their entire lives. This particular ugly baby was also piping loud, her cries as piercing as those of furious gulls. She could not be comforted. Not even her mother's milky breast nor the warm swaddling in which she was wrapped calmed her. The mother, exhausted by her long travail, gave her ugly daughter the only thing she could, a name of power, Ide, 'thirsts for goodness and knowledge.'

Shortly after feeding and holding her ugly daughter, the mother slipped into a deep sleep. The midwife could see it was no ordinary sleep, but one so deep that she could not feel the mother's pulse. She held the polished blade of a silver knife under the mother's nose. The comatose woman's exhalations misted the shiny blade.

The midwife slumped in relief, her patient still alive. For now, at least. She rocked the beautiful babe and the ugly one in turn, and bade the miller to find a wet nurse nearby and bring her hence.

The labour continued—the midwife could see the mother's hard round belly ripple as the third baby struggled to be born—but the mother's eyes remained closed. She hovered somewhere between life and death all through the night and into the next day. The midwife kept checking the mother's breathing, kept feeling for a pulse, kept trying to rouse her.

At dawn on April third, the silver knife blade no longer fogged when placed under the mother's nose. Yet the third baby still struggled and pushed inside her womb. The midwife used her knife to cut the mother from breastbone to groin. It took time and care to saw through the layers of skin, flesh, and muscle without hurting the baby trapped inside the corpse, but the midwife, while old, was strong and skilled and determined to save the babe's life if she could. She did.

When the midwife held the third baby up to the light, she could see that like the eldest of the triplets, the youngest daughter was also beautiful, albeit in a different way. This last baby had golden skin, deep dark eyes like a shadowed winters' pond, and a full head of hair, blue-black and glossy as a raven's wing. She nursed enthusiastically from her mothers' still-warm body.

The midwife knew nothing of the power and magic of naming, so she called the babe simply Ciara, 'dark'. She told the miller that his wife had named the child with her last breath.

The wet nurse, Sarah, grew to love the three girls as much as her own baby boy, Hugh. The miller noted this and married the wet nurse by the time the babes were weaned. Why not, after all? His daughters needed a mother, the wet nurse needed work and a place to live with her son, and the mill needed extra hands. This way the neighbours would finally stop trying to fix him up with all the unmarried scolds in their families.

An unexpected boon for John was that his new wife, Sarah, was the daughter of a brewer, so understood how to make beer. Her skill thrilled thrifty John, as it was another way to use the grist left behind in the bedstone after the grain had been milled; another way to make money.

For the next sixteen years, John and Sarah and their blended family lived lives of increasing prosperity and relative harmony. Hugh became John's apprentice. Etain, Ide, and Ciara learned brewing-craft from their step-mother and took it in turns to sell beer from a stall on market days.

Hugh grew up tall and straw-haired, a strong young man of almost eighteen. He was already a journeyman miller, helping his step-father in all aspects of the work. A quiet young man, he protected his step-sisters from any insult, with his fists, if necessary.

Etain and Ciara, at sixteen, had straight backs and graceful bearing. Both were famed for their beauty. Etain had grown up bright as the sun, golden hair to her knees. She oiled it and brushed it one hundred times every day. She was patient in this, as she was in nothing else. Some said her blue eyes reminded them of the mantle of Mary, Mother of God.

Ciara's beauty rivalled that of her sister's, but in another form: coal-black hair, straight brows, and flashing dark eyes like a winter storm. Ciara had been a child of strong emotion, and young womanhood had only enhanced this. At ten, Ciara told her parents that when it came time for her to marry, she would only accept a love-match. Even then, John and Sarah knew Ciara was resolute. Some said Ciara's mood—be it foul or fair—could form the weather for the entire village.

The village gossips agreed that if the parents were clever and canny, both girls would marry well. Then, having thoroughly discussed the marriage prospects of the beautiful sisters, their talk would inevitably turn to poor Ide. All the old women agreed, Ide would never marry.

As the midwife had predicted, Ide remained as bald as a babe. Her lack of brows and eyelashes gave her a curious countenance, similar to that of a rabbit. Her left hip sat higher than the right, giving her a pronounced limp. Working in the brewery and hauling half-kegs to the village on market days had given her solid muscles in her arms and back, so solid that thick ropey veins bulged in her forearms. Her skin was plagued with swarms of small red boils. When she spoke or laughed, she held a demure hand over her mouth so none could see the snarl of square yellow teeth.

The gossips agreed that while terrifically ugly, Ide was a strong, clever girl, hard-working, a girl who loved God and never complained. It was a shame she would never marry. The gossips felt certain that in the minds of men, beauty is more important than virtue. They nodded at one another wisely over their cups of buttermilk and mead.

The old women had only one criticism of Ide: she did not seem to care that she was ugly. If anyone—drunken louts at her beer stall on market days, for example—mentioned the fact, Ide merely shrugged.

If they jeered at her, she responded, "I am what the Lord God made me; the likes of you should not question it."

If they pestered her further, she would box their ears and deny their custom. "If I be too ugly, so too is the work of my hand. Far too ugly a beer for a pretty man like you to drink. Be off with ye."

Most louts would skulk away, grumbling under their breath to their fellows.

The occasional woman-hater who raised his hand to Ide had to deal with Hugh and his sunburned fists. Hugh loved his sisters. He fought to protect them. He never lost.

Ide drew attention to herself in other ways. For example, the linen kerchief Ide wore tied around her shiny round head was bright red. Her kirtle, while modestly cut, was the same shocking red. She even wore red leather shoes.

The old women felt that it was bad enough when comely women made spectacles of themselves with bright colours; to them it seemed perverse that an ugly woman would draw attention to herself.

"No good will come from all tha'", the gossips agreed.

Chapter Two

On the day the letter arrived, Ide was mucking out the chicken house, her mind adrift. Of all the sisters, Ide was the one who didn't mind dirty work, so caring for the chickens had long been Ide's task. The birds amused Ide with their button bright eyes and skeptical expressions. She sang softly to them as she worked, thinking of everything-and-nothing all at once.

A rapping on the frame of the chicken house's open door startled Ide from her reverie. She looked up.

Ciarra, out of breath, stood in the doorway. "Did you not hear us calling you from the house?" she gasped.

Over Ciara's shoulder, Ide could see Etain pelting towards the chicken house, blonde hair streaming behind her in ribbons, gleaming in the sun.

"Sorry, sister, I did not. What's happening?" Ide raised the forehead skin where her brows should be. "Whatever it is, it has certainly excited Etain."

Ciara smiled. "A new hairbrush excites Etain. This isn't excitement, this is a . . . a . .. frenzy." She followed Ide's gaze. "Well, she's almost here. I'll let her tell it." Ciara's storm-dark eyes were unreadable.

"Ide!" panted Etain, "Did she tell you yet?"

"No," Ciara answered for Ide. "I left that for you." Ciara leaned against the outside of the chicken house, stones warm against her back. Always a creature of the evening, she sought the shadow cast by the overhang of the thatched roof.

Etain shook the piece of parchment grasped in her left fist, "He wants to marry me!" Light danced in Etain's sea-blue eyes and her broad grin showed every one of her straight pearly teeth.

Ide wiped her hands on her apron and stepped out of the chicken house. She covered her mouth as she spoke to Etain.

"Who? Who wants to marry you?"

Etain rattled the parchment she clutched. "William, son of William, miller on the River Foyle!" Etain was trembling with the effort of keeping her feet still.

"Let me look," said Ide as she snatched the parchment from her blonde sister's hand.

Etain pranced in place like an eager pony, excited eyes on Ide's face. Ciara was still and silent in her shadow.

Though all of John and Sarah's children could read, Ide was the most skilled, especially when reading out loud. She never hesitated over new words. To her sisters, Ide read:

John Bann,
The Mill near the mouth of the River Bann, Ulster

May 1st, 1673.

Sir—

It gives me pleasure to inform you that my eldest son, William, heir to my Mill at the River Foyle, and other Properties, has agreed to marry your daughter, Etain.

Your letter of last month making a Proposal to unite our two families, families already united by a shared trade, caught me by surprise. Nevertheless, I look favourably on your offer. My son has long desired a wife, the dowry you offer is generous, and tales of your daughter's beauty have long since reached us in Carrigan.

Forgive me for the asking, but my son (who is also named William) beseeches me to confirm the offer of marriage and dowry is for your eldest daughter, Etain?

I have already reassured him and shown him your letter where you mention Etain by name, but he is concerned that the dowry is too generous to accompany a beautiful wife. Forgive him, he is brash, as are many young men. I am sure you must remember this from your own youth.

If the offer is for Etain's hand, my William enthusiastically accepts.

I remain respectfully yours,

William Foyle,
Village of Carrigan, Ulster.

Mouth screened by her hand, Ide licked her lips and considered what to say. A moment passed. Etain looked first at

Ide standing in the open doorway of the chicken house, then Ciara standing in its shadow.

At last, Ide spoke.

"Congratulations on your upcoming nuptials, sister. I would embrace you but for worry of your clothes." She gestured at her apron smeared with all the filth of the chicken house, and smiled at Etain from behind her hand.

Etain nodded at Ide, then turned her gaze to Ciara standing in the shadow.

"And you, Sister? Will you congratulate me on my engagement?"

"That depends. Are you happy to be auctioned off to the highest bidder?" snapped Ciara.

Ide's stomach twisted, and she grimaced. Not this fight again.

"I've got to finish my work," Ide remarked, to no one in particular. She walked back inside the malodorous chicken house and continued shovelling.

She tried to focus on the clucking sounds of the chickens, but her sisters' argument continued on the threshold:

"I knew that you'd be jealous! You never let me enjoy anything!" accused Etain.

Then Ciara's voice, low, measured, somehow dangerous. "I am not jealous of you, Etain. I simply think a woman should pick her own husband, for love, and not be sold by her parents like a sheep at auction. Have you no respect for yourself?"

"Oh!" exclaimed Etain. "You just say that because no one is asking for your hand, you . . . you . . . vampire!"

Ide heard Etain burst into angry tears, and the sound of Etain's soft-soled shoes as she turned in the gravel to run back to the house.

Silence, except for a few clucks from disapproving hens.

"Ciara," said Ide.

"Yes."

"Can you help me with the mucking out? Two pairs of hands makes short work, and I have bread to bake and beer to brew before sunset."

Ciara appeared in the doorway. "I will help you."

She rolled up her sleeves and knotted her skirt up and out of the way of all the filth.

The two worked in silence until the task was done. Ide noticed that at the start Ciara's movements were abrupt, almost violent, and her dark eyes were sometimes glossy with tears. By the time the chicken house was clean and strewn with fresh hay, and the manure carried away to the compost heap, Ciara was filthy but no longer upset.

Ide and Ciara headed to the river to wash.

Watching her sister's face, Ide ventured, "I know you are not jealous of Etain. It's a matter of principle; you've always said so."

The worried knot between Ciara's brows loosened and she breathed deep. "Thank you. I am glad you understand. If mother and father think they can auction off one of us, they'll auction off all of us."

Not me. Out loud, Ide said, "Perhaps mother and father have done this because they know Etain does not mind? She is in love with the idea of love, but that doesn't mean real love will not come to her and this William in time. You and Etain are not the same; Mother and Father know you cannot be treated the same. I think you will be able to select your own husband, when you meet him."

Ciara sighed. "You are always so reasonable, Ide. Why do you never get angry at . . . all this?" Ciara made an expansive gesture toward their home, the mill, the chicken house, the pen full of white cows with red ears. Ide knew that Ciara was really gesturing at Ide's face and body.

"I am not angry because I accept this is what God has planned for me; besides, there is no way to change anything, so what's the point of wishing?"

Ide shrugged as she stripped off her apron and knelt on it at the riverside. She retrieved a sliver of soap from her dress pocket and started lathering her hands and forearms in the river. She handed the soap to Ciara as Ciara, too, knelt to wash.

Ciara thought for a moment, frowning. " 'What's the point of wishing for love'? We all deserve love, Ide."

"Maybe, but 'wishing' and 'getting' are not the same thing, for some."

Ciara reddened to the hairline. No one in the family ever discussed Ide's appearance with Ide, but all of them referred to it obliquely. Whenever Ide herself referred to it, the others felt embarrassed.

"You don't know what the future holds, Ide."

Now it was Ide's turn to sigh. "Very well, you are right. I am no witch, I cannot see the future."

Months later, Ide would remember making this remark, and wish she had been a witch. A witch might have been able to stop events. As it was, life ground forward, ever forward, heavy like the great stone in the mill, and just as relentless.

Chapter Three

A month before the wedding, William Foyle the younger arrived at the mill on the River Bann. He was tall, thick with muscle, and very sunburned from his travels from Carrigan. His blonde hair was bleached almost white by the sun, his navy blue eyes a startling contrast.

Etain's eyes sparkled from the moment she laid eyes on William. William merely looked relieved that Etain was Etain, and not Ide. William could never meet Ide's gaze, and often spoke as though Ide was not present.

The two sets of parents had agreed that young William should have a chance to get to know his betrothed and her family before the wedding, and assist with all the preparations for taking the bride and her dowry back to Corrigan.

William Foyle the elder and his wife stayed behind in Corrigan to oversee the building of a small cottage for the newlyweds. They would come to see the wedding ceremony and enjoy the wedding feast.

The Bann family housed Etain's fiancé in the loft of the mill house with Hugh.

"Propriety's sake, young man, the town gossips, you see, nothing personal, though the accommodations are rather rude," John had told young William.

"Not a problem, sir, plenty of time for that later, after the wedding."

John had chuckled and slapped William on the back, then helped the young man carry a second feather-mattress upstairs to the mill-loft. William would sleep on it by himself until the wedding, and then take it with him back to Corrigan as part of the marriage dowry, along with his bride.

John Bann had mischaracterized the conditions of the mill-loft, a bit of father-in-lawish humble-bragging. Ever since Hugh had been fourteen, he'd opted to sleep in the mill loft rather than the family house. In the four years since Hugh had made this change, he'd taken care to make the loft a comfortable place. Etain, Ide, and Ciara had even made him a rug woven from rags and knit Hugh extra thick socks so he was comfortable in the mill-loft no matter the weather.

Whenever anyone asked him why he slept in the loft, Hugh always said the same thing—I need my privacy—but Ide had never believed him. She had long noted how Hugh's eyes followed Ciara as she moved around the house, how Hugh would sometimes bring home wildflowers along with rabbit or fowl when he'd been off hunting and trapping. Hugh always gave the wildflowers to Ciara.

Only Ide noticed Hugh's gaze, and only Ide saw significance in the gift of flowers. Ide had considered mentioning something to Ciara but decided against it. She probably doesn't notice it because every man except father looks at her the same way; it might be better for her to never notice. Ide was of the opinion that great beauty is as much a curse as great ugliness.

The first Sunday after young William Foyle arrived, he gave Etain a few presents: soft suede gloves, a tortoiseshell comb for her hair, and a gold ring set with a blue stone. She was to wear it on the ring finger of her right hand until the wedding day to show that she was spoken for. Ide felt the banns being read at church for the three Sundays before the wedding was likely enough notice for everyone, particularly in the light of village gossip, but never mind. Etain loves trinkets; she loves it when people fuss over her. It makes her happy.

At the end of the wedding ceremony, William would move it from her right ring finger to her left ring finger to symbolize their union. Ide had heard many old women say there is a vein that runs straight from the heart to the left ring finger. Some even said that if a wife lied to her husband, the right ring finger would shrivel and turn black.

Ide kept her own counsel on this, and continued to bake bread, muck out the chicken house, sell beer on market days, and sew household linens for Etain's dowry. She had more work than usual. Even Ciara had been pressed into service with wedding preparations.

Hugh also had some extra tasks in preparation, building long trestle tables and benches for the wedding feast. William had explained how the Foyles were bringing half of Corrigan with them to the festivities. John and Sarah Bann had winced at the extra expense, smiled at their future son-in-law, and increased the prices for beer and milling.

William, to Ide's surprise, was not an empty-headed lout. She had feared the worst for her sister. While initially cool toward him, both Ide and Ciara grew friendlier toward him. William had the opposite effect on Hugh, who grew cooler and more distant as the wedding day approached.

Ide was puzzled. So one Saturday morning as she and Hugh pulled a trolley full of beer in barrels to market, she asked him about it.

"You seemed to like William when he first arrived here," observed Ide.

Hugh's eyes widened in response, but he nodded slowly.

"But less and less as the weeks have gone on."

Hugh shrugged, and turned his red face away to look at something on the horizon.

Ide paused, waiting for Hugh to collect himself. Voice quiet, she asked, "Has something happened between you two? An argument, perhaps?"

Hugh turned his head to meet Ide's gaze. "Between him and me, nothing's happened. He seems a decent sort, maybe a bit fancier than pleases me, but well enough suited to Etain, as she puts on airs as well."
"You're right, she does, but it's harmless. Give her vanity a light petting, and she's as pleasant as pie."

Hugh shrugged. His face settled into a grim cast.

Ide said, "There's more. There is something you are not telling me."

Hugh pressed his lips together in a thin line and shook his head.

Ide continued to walk on in silence. In Ide's experience, most people were dying to tell secrets. Secrets are bigger than one soul can comfortably hold.

Hugh sighed and dropped his cart handle. He paced back and forth, scowling.

"Is it about Ciara?"

Hugh stopped mid-pace, face white underneath his sunburn. "What about Ciara?" he asked, suspicion in his voice.

Ide faced Hugh and looked him in the eye. "I know you are in love with Ciara. I know that's why you moved your bed to the mill-loft, so you would not have to sleep under a roof so close to her."

Emotions blew across Hugh's face like clouds on a stormy day. His mouth dry, he croaked, "Who else knows?"

"No one. Not even Ciara; every man but Father looks at her the way you look at her, so I think she may not know what it signifies."

"What about Etaine?"

"Etaine is not a person who observes others. She pays attention to who is looking at her."

"But not you; you watch everything." Hugh's resentment was palpable. "Are you going to tell anyone?"

"Why would I? Mother and Father have their own concerns. Etain notices little. Ciara has no idea. Telling any of them would simply make them unhappy. You've taken steps to put distance between Ciara and yourself. Soon she will marry and live elsewhere, I am sure. So who exactly is there to tell, and what should I be telling?"

Hugh picked up his cart handle and started to trudging toward town with their wares. Ide stepped quickly to keep up with him.

Hugh cleared his throat, then spat into the dirt. "Here's what there is to tell." He started to sing: "I courted one with gloves and rings, but love thee above all things, fa-la-la-la-la-la-la-di-dah."

"A song? I've never heard that song."

"No one has. Weeping William just wrote it yesterday." Ide was nonplussed. "So?"

"I overheard Weeping William singing it to Ciara last night, under the moon. He was holding her hand, and they were making cow eyes at each other."

Ide stopped trudging, dropped the cart handle and hands on her hips, faced Hugh. "Tell me everything, Hugh. And start from the beginning."

Hugh sighed. "I wish we could stop and tap one of those kegs."

"We can stop if you like, for a rest, but let's leave the kegs alone for now."

Hugh squared his shoulders. They dragged the cart off to one side of the lane, so if a rider or someone else with a wagon or cart needed to pass, they could. They sat lane-side and kept an eye on their wares while Hugh spoke.

"When William first got here, he seemed a decent bloke. He was pleasant company when we were alone at night in the loft, did his share of work, and Etain is clearly head-over-heels for him."

"Go on . . ."

"As we got to know each other better, he told me about his worries and his troubles. On the way here he was very afraid that Etain . . ." Hugh started to blush and stammer.
"Would look like me, the bald, pimpled, snaggle-toothed witch of the Bann," Ide finished.

Tears welled up in Hugh's eyes. "Don't say it like that. No one that knows you would be so cruel. It's just that the gossips . . ."

"Have nothing better to do all day than spin yarns of my great ugliness. And apparently manage to spread their tales all over Ulster."

"I'm so sorry, Ide." Hugh's flushed face and brimming eyes were sincere.

Ide's eyes were dry, her back erect, her tone no-nonsense. "I know all these things, Hugh. Tell me what I don't know: why do you call him 'Weeping William' and what is going on between Ciara and him?"

Hugh toyed with a twig he'd found, using his thumbnails to skin the bark from it. Staring at his hands as he peeled, Hugh said, "After he'd been here about a week, I'd hear him weeping in the middle of the night. At first, I thought maybe I was dreaming, but after a few nights, it was clear he was distraught. On the fourth night, I sat up in bed and said, 'either tell me what's bothering you or go do that somewhere else.' I expected him to flounce away from the mill-loft, insulted. Instead, he poured out his heart to me."

"And?"

"And he confessed that when he first arrived, he was pleased that Etain was his betrothed, but after a few days—his words, mind—'she lost her sparkle for me'."

"What does that mean?"

"It means that when faced with the choice between a beautiful but vain and empty-headed woman and a beautiful, headstrong, and passionate one, he prefers the latter."

No one will ever feel like that about me. I'm not sure if that is tragic, or a tremendous stroke of luck. "Right, so he spent enough time with all of us as a family to realize that he prefers Ciara, even though he's betrothed to Etain."

"Yes, and that's why he was weeping and writing poems and songs. I thought that would be the end of it, that he'd do his duty to Etain, live in Corrigan, and we'd hear no more. But then, a few nights ago, I woke while the mill-loft was still black as pitch. I listened, but I could not hear William's breathing. The harder I listened, the more I was certain he wasn't in the mill-loft with me. But I could hear a thin voice singing somewhere outside."

"Singing?"

"Yes. I crept from the loft and tried to follow the sound. I carried no candle, for the clouds had moved, a sliver of moon lit my way."

"What did you see, Hugh?"

"The two of them, sitting side-by-side on the bank of the Bann, looking at the swans swim in the moonlight. He was singing some romantic nonsense to her and stroking her hair. When he stopped singing, she sighed and kissed him on the mouth." Tears dripped from Hugh's cheeks; he covered his face with his gnarled, work-hardened hands.

Ide placed a steadying hand on Hugh's shoulder, her heart full of Hugh's pain. "So you love the step-sister you cannot have; she loves the man betrothed to our other sister, who in turn loves the idea of marriage to a handsome, well-heeled man."

Hugh nodded and snuffled back his tears. "What's more, they've been out walking every night while the rest of us sleep. Last night, after he sang to her, they agreed that after church on Sunday, William would tell Father that he wants to marry Ciara, not Etain." He paused, to swallow the lump in his throat. "He's going to break Etain's heart, then marry Ciara and take her away forever!"

Ide put her arms around her brother and rocked him gently as he wept. She said a silent prayer: "Mother Mary, preserve us all. Help Hugh find love with another. And please, find a way for my sisters to be happy."

After a while, Hugh snuffled again, wiped his eyes on his shirt sleeve and said, "Well, let's get on with it. There is beer to sell at market."

Ide stood up, dusted off her skirts, and started to pull on her cart handle. As best she could, she put what Hugh had said out of mind. *No sense in worrying over something I cannot control. The best I can do is pray. It will all come to a head in a few days. The marriage—if it happens—is just a week away.*

Chapter Four

While Ide and Hugh were away selling beer at market, Ciara announced she was going into the forest to pick mushrooms, and Mother and Father had gone to town to speak with someone about . . . something. Etain wasn't listening when they told her where they were going or why.

She sat in the sun, embroidering the nightgown she wanted to wear on her wedding night. She was half in a dream, imagining the spectacle of her marriage procession and ceremony. She could not imagine having a more handsome or sensitive husband than William. What's more, William had exquisite taste; she had never seen a finer pair of suede gloves than the ones he gave to her, nor a tortoiseshell comb more delicately crafted. And the ring! The ring itself was so beautiful that Etain wondered if it had been wrought by angels.

Etain hummed to herself as she sewed. When she was finished with the nightgown, she would make William's grooms' shirt.

Etain felt eyes upon her, so she looked up. There was William, standing in the open door of the house. She was not sure how long he'd been there, watching her. She performed a quick mental check: were her skirts arranged prettily? Did her gold hair gleam in the sunlight? She thought so. She smiled at William, waving him over.

William joined her on her blanket. His face was set in tense lines, but that made him even more handsome in Etain's opinion- more a man than a boy. He took her left hand, the hand that held the nightgown.

"I must speak my mind to you, Etain."

Etain smiled. "You find that you love me so and cannot wait to make me your own? It is just another week you must wait, sirrah," she said, teasing. Her blue eyes sparkled.

William did not smile at this jest. His grip on her left hand tightened. "No, now you must listen to me. What I must tell you is serious."

Etain felt a sudden chill despite the warm sun on her skin. "Dearest, whatever is the matter, are you ill? Why such a grave countenance?" Her palms started to sweat despite the chill she felt.

"I wanted to tell you . . . tell you before I told your Father and mine . . ." William cleared his throat, and his eyes darted from side-to-side like an animal looking for escape. "I wanted to tell you that I must break our engagement."

Etain felt like she'd fallen off a fast-moving horse— winded, numb. She shook her head and pretended bravado she didn't feel. "Don't be silly, my darling. It's all arranged." *Perhaps he is teasing me?*

William sighed. He squeezed Etain's left hand in both of his, crumpling the fine linen nightgown.

"Please, please, just listen to me."

Eyes rounded with fear, Etain nodded.

"Etain, I cannot marry you. I love another."

"What?!"

"I cannot marry you. I love a different lady."

Etain flushed a hot circle on each lovely cheek. "Love! Some whore in Corrigan? A fat milkmaid? Who?" she sputtered.

William winced. "I'm sorry, Etain. I love your sister, Ciara."

Etain went still, eyes unblinking as she stared at William.

A long moment passed.

William cleared his throat again. "Ciara and I will tell your Father about this tomorrow after church, then ride directly to Corrigan. Ciara and I will marry there, to save you the embarrassment. Tell whatever story you wish about our broken engagement, that you refused me—whatever you like."

Etain looked at the gleaming embroidery needle she held in her right hand. She looked at William's handsome, earnest face.

Swift and sure, she plunged the embroidery needle into the meaty part of his left cheek, as deeply as she could while gripping its end between thumb and forefinger.

William let go of her, but he made no sound. He brought his hands to his face. He placed his hands over Etain's and forced her to ease the needle from his face.

Voice just a whisper, William said, "I understand. I am sorry. Please tell your family I must be away for the night, but I shall join everyone at church in the morning."

He walked away from Etain without a backwards glance, heading in the direction of the stable and his horse.

Etain stared at the blood-smeared needle in her hand. Drops of blood and tears fell onto the snowy linen nightgown. If that can't be my nightdress for my wedding night, then perhaps it should be Ciara's shroud.

An hour later, Etain was chopping vegetables for the night's meal, Mother's big kitchen knife in her hand. She worked quickly, making neat piles of onion, carrot, fresh herbs. No one had returned home yet, and the sun was still high in the cloudless June sky.

She heard Ciara's soft-soled shoes kiss the stone of the threshold. In that moment, Etain's speculative plans solidified.

"Hellooo!" called out Ciara.

"In here!" replied Etain, voice cool and musical.

Ciara entered the kitchen with a large basket of morels. "I found so many. Maybe we can eat some tonight and dry the rest for winter."

Etain nodded. "Good idea."

"Is everything fine, Etain? You seem . . . odd."

"Yes, I'm fine. I think the strain on my eyes from all the sewing has given me a headache," she said, as she pinched the bridge of her nose in mock pain.

"Well, fresh air or willow bark, that's what Mother always says for a headache."

"Good idea. Fresh air, I think. I'd like to walk by the river for a bit. Come with me?"

Ciara hesitated. *No doubt wondering if William has talked to me, or if he hasn't, she's wondering whether she dare risk speaking with me for fear of giving away their secret.*

Etain put down her knife, covered the chopped vegetables with a clean length of linen, and wiped her hands on her apron.

"Come, sister, we have few walks together in our future. In just over a week, I'll be living over hill and dale. Soon I'll have babies tugging at my skirts. Walk with me while you still can."

Ciara cocked her head, drew her brows together for a moment. She exhaled. "All right," she said, "A last walk by our river. Perhaps we will see the swans."

"It could be. Let us hope. Bring your basket; we may see more mushrooms on our way."

Etain linked elbows with Ciara, and they walked to the shore of the River Bann, then followed the bank toward the northern sea. They picked mushrooms on the way.

At first, Etain could feel that Ciara's body was tense with undefined worry. *She does not want to be found out. She hopes*

122

to slip away with my husband like a thief in the night. Etain felt something bubble inside her, but she breathed deep and quashed it.

After ten minutes of walking, Etain felt Ciara's muscles start to relax. Perfect. Etain unlinked arms and walked over to the edge of the river bank. A brisk wind carried the salt and dead fish smells from the ocean strand. They were that close to where the Bann met the ocean.

"Come look at this!" she called to Ciara, pointing down into the river.

Ciara hesitated for a second. Every nerve in Etain's body sang with tension.

"What is it? What do you see?" asked Ciara as she stood near Etain on the river bank.
"Just look where I am pointing, in the river, just under the surface."

"What am I looking for?" Ciara asked, turning away from Etain to look at the place Etain pointed.

Etain pushed Ciara with all her strength, all her rage. "A drowned liar, sister-love!"
Ciara went headfirst into the Bann. The river was not at its deepest here, so close to the sea, but it was deeper than Ciara was tall. The current was strong, and her water-soaked skirts were heavy, dragging her down. Sometimes Ciara sank; sometimes she swam.

Flailing her arms, bobbing and coughing river water, Ciara cried, "Sister, reach to me your hand!"

Etain smirked. "I'm your sister now, am I? What was I when you were stealing my husband-to-be?"

"Please, please let me live. Help me! Help me, and all that's mine I'll surely give!"

"It's your own true love I'll have, and more!" spat Etain. She noticed a few fist-sized rocks on the bank. She picked up one of these, took careful aim, and tossed it. The rock hit Ciara in the forehead. The cut wasn't big, but it bled profusely. Ciara's flailing continued, but with less energy.

Etain threw the rest of the stones at Ciara, one by one, until Ciara's head no longer broke the water.

"You will never come ashore," whispered Etain. Ciara's lifeless body floated face down, caught in the current of the Bann. Her mushroom basket floated next to her. *Dead she floats as gracefully as a swan. No ugly flailing and mewling; being drowned suits her.*

Etain smiled to herself as the river current bore her sister's body to the ocean. *I've got to beat the rest of them home.*

Etain took off at a run.

Chapter Five

By dark, everyone was worried about Ciara. The family did not know William's whereabouts, either, but Etain pointed out that Ciara had left for the forest without William.

"You think she's out in the forest, at night, by herself?" Hugh asked.

"It's possible," said Ide. "She might have twisted an ankle or had some other small mishap."

Hugh announced, "I'm not waiting for that ninnyhammer William to prance home when Ciara might be in danger. Even if he is with her in the forest, he could be overwhelmed by robbers or . . ." His voice broke.

"You have the right of it, son. Let's away," said Father.

Father, Hugh and the men they could gather along the way searched for Ciara in the forest in the dark, with torches. Just before dawn, after a few hours' sleep, they got up and did it again. They found no trace of Ciara in the forest. When the rest of the family left for church, Father and Hugh stayed at home, in case Ciara somehow returned home on her own.

When Mother, Ide, and Etain arrived at church, they spotted William, who stood on the church steps, searching the crowd.

"Where's Ciara?" William asked.

Mother started to cry. Etain's face was a frozen mask: pale, drawn, eyes downcast.

Ide placed her hand on William's forearm and met his gaze. "She did not come home from the forest yesterday."

"What?"

"She went to pick mushrooms and did not come home. Men have been searching . . ."

William interrupted, "Who is searching? Where?"

"Father, Hugh, other men. In the forest near the mill . . ."

Before Ide could finish, William shoved his way through the church-goers, off to where his horse was tied. Moments later, he galloped past the crowd without a backward look, even though Etain, ashen-faced, waved her handkerchief at him.

When Etain noticed that Ide was looking at her, Etain remarked, "Family is very important to him. He is going to be an excellent husband to me."

Ide put her arm around Mother's shoulders to comfort the older woman, and acknowledged her sister's words with a reserved nod. She drew her brows together over her nose. *Something is afoot here, but I know not what.*

Chapter Six

Just before Sunday supper, fishermen found Ciara's dead body and her empty mushroom basket. They carried her remains back to the family's home.

When the fishermen arrived with the body, Mother started to wail and tear at her hair. Ide asked the men to lay Ciara's body on the work table in the mill loft, out of sight.

When Father, Hugh, and William returned, the family wept together.

As darkness was falling, Ide pulled Hugh aside.

"Hugh, I am sorry, but Ciara, I mean, her body, is laid out in your loft. We'll need a place to wash her and prepare her for burial. Take my bed; sleep will not come for me tonight; I am certain of it," said Ide.

Hugh's tear-smeared face was red and swollen. His nose was stuffed up. He blew it on his handkerchief.

Hugh said, "I know it is women's work, Ide, work that will likely fall to you. I want to help you. I want to say goodbye."

Tears welled up in Hugh's eyes again, and he dabbed at his nose.

Ide was taken aback. Hugh's request struck her as, if not obscene, certainly improper. She shook her head.
She said, "Hugh, we can't do that."

Hugh's face fell, but he nodded and turned away to climb the stairs to Ide's room. His steps were slow and heavy.

When Ide returned to the kitchen, she saw that Etain and William had gone off somewhere, and her father and stepmother sat in silence, holding hands over the kitchen table, tears sliding silently over their cheeks.

"Father, Mother, I will prepare her. When do you want to . . ."

"Bury her?" asked father, his voice hoarse with suffering. It brought a lump to Ide's own throat to hear it, but there was no time for that. There was work to be done.

Father squeezed his wife's hand. He said, "I think we need to do it fast, maybe late in the day tomorrow. There is still so much to do for the wedding."

Mother nodded.

"You mean we are still going through with the wedding, even though . . ." Ide gestured uselessly.

"Yes," said Mother, "that's how Ciara would have wanted it."

Ide nodded. *But would she, though? Hardly likely, given what Hugh had to say about William courting Ciara.*
After supper, Ide went alone to the mill loft to see about washing and preparing Ciara's body. This proved to be a daunting task, as Ide had to stop from time to time to weep for her sister. Eventually Ide fell asleep on Hugh's bed, exhausted from tension and sorrow.

128

But sleep was not restorative for Ide. Instead she dreamed, wild uncomfortable dreams with shrieking wind, lashings of rain, and the sound of the surf crashing on the beach. Ide was pursuing a hooded, cloaked figure on the sea strand. Ide felt, with the logic of dreams, that if only she could catch up to the cloaked figure, the storm would stop. She ran and ran, sometimes dreaming that her fingertips brushed the coarse fabric of the cloak, but she was never able to grip it in her fist. Even in dreams, her uneven hips ached if she moved too quickly. Running made it feel as though her hip joints were full of broken glass.

Frustrated by the effort, Ide shouted, "Who are you? What do you want?"

She was almost close enough to grab the figure.

The figure turned around, slipping the hood off.

"Ciara!" called Ide. "Let me speak with you. Can it be that you still live somehow?"

Ciara's face was pale, and her lips were tinged blue. Her forehead bore a long red gash that did not bleed. She shook her head. A tear slid down her left cheek.

"But your shade must be coming to me for a reason. What is it, tell me."

Ciara's ghost opened her mouth, but no sound came out.

Ide touched Ciara's shoulder, and was surprised to find it solid beneath her hand. Dreams are curious places.

Ciara's shade leaned forward and cupped Ide's cheek. When the icy fingers touched her face, Ide could see a dream within this dream, events playing out before her mind's eye. She saw herself washing Ciara's dead body, she saw herself cutting into Ciara's chest, all the while a song repeated in her mind. Distracted by the gory sights of this dream within a dream, Ide heard the line "Ide made a harp from her breast bone" again and again.

She woke in a cold sweat, hip joints burning from the running she had done in her dream. Hugh was shaking her by the shoulder.

"I thought no sleep would come for you, sister," said Hugh.

"I'm just as surprised as you," said Ide. "I dreamed, but I think it was no natural dream."

Ide described her experience to Hugh, ending with the part about the breast bone.

"Is this real or just the fancy of a grieving mind?" asked Hugh.

"I don't know," said Ide.

"So, what are you going to do?"

"Whatever I do, it must be tonight, for Father and Mother want to bury her on the morrow."

Hugh scoffed. "Nothing should intrude on that damned wedding, eh, Ide?"

He shook his head.

Ide sighed and rubbed her eyes. "I don't want to be faced with a reproachful shade every night for the rest of my days because I didn't follow instructions."

"So you are considering it?"

"Yes. If I do, can you help me?" Ide asked.

Hugh wrapped his arms around his middle and started to pace across the mill-loft floor. "I'm not sure . . ." he whispered. "I loved her so much, I don't think I can . . . cut into her."

So it was that Hugh left the mill-loft while Ide worked. She sliced through clammy cold flesh, and snapped bones with her gore-smeared hands. Removing the breast bone and flensing the flesh from it took more than an hour.

She filled the chest cavity with sawdust, and secured the rest of the remains with cloth bindings from waist to throat, similar to the way one swaddles a colicky infant: tightly wound, with multiple layers. Then she dressed the body in the dress Ciara had made herself for Etain and William's wedding, a simple high-necked gown the colour of claret. She brushed Ciara's long black hair until it gleamed in the candlelight.

When Hugh returned just after dawn, the body was clean, dressed, and appeared no different than one that still had its breastbone. Ide and Hugh reckoned that no one would inspect

Ciara's body too closely, as the weather was warm, and the body was already starting to smell.

"What will we use for strings on this harp?" asked Hugh.

"I had not thought that far yet, brother," replied Ide.

Hugh stoked Ciara's hair. Tears welled in his eyes, but when he spoke, his voice was calm and steady. "We can use strands of her hair."

Ide was not sure what Hugh proposed would work, but she reckoned there was no harm in trying.

"I will leave you to make the harp strings, then. I am going to boil the harp . . . er . . . frame near the chicken house, to clean it. Then we must get busy with preparations for the wake after the funeral."

"As you say, sister. Though I think a funeral in the same week that Etain and Weeping Wiliam wed is a bad omen."

"There is naught to be done for it. Let's get on with our work."

Chapter Seven

The wedding procession and then the ceremony on the church steps lasted an eternity, or so thought Ide. The bride seemed more brittle and manic than she did happy. The bridegroom was clearly preoccupied. But at last the deed was done: Etain and William were wife and husband. Everyone made their way back to the Mill House on the River Bann for the wedding feast.

The women bustled in and out of the house, bringing delicious dishes to the table: a whole roast pig, several geese baked into pies, and all manner of vegetables. Tapped kegs of beer stood nearby. Ide and Mother had been busy since Ciara's wake. The sturdy tables Hugh had built for the feast groaned under the weight of all the food.

Most of the men were seated already, but children still ran about. William and Etain sat at the table's head. Etain clasped one of William's hands in both of hers, but he did not meet her gaze. Instead, he stared off into the distance, his face drawn and shuttered like a disused building.

Father stood behind them. He addressed the crowd:

"Welcome to the wedding feast for William and Etain. Please everyone be seated!"

There was a great bustling as women ushered children to the table.

"It is with a glad heart that I welcome William as my son-in-law; having him join the family and seeing Etain happily wed goes some way to ease our other sorrows," Father said. "Let us start with a prayer of thanks for this wedding and this food and then . . ."

He paused.

"Am I hearing music?"

The guests around the tables looked this way and that. There was music.

The harp, standing on the table in front of Hugh's place, was playing by itself. At first the music was soft, but as more people realized its origin, the music grew louder, as though drawing energy from their attention. The crowd was silent in the wonder of it all.

The sun emerged from behind a passing cloud. The sunlight on the polished bone of the harp frame made it glow, and the raven-black strings glittered. The harp played and sang in an alto voice:

As one grew bright, just like the sun
So coal black grew the younger one

A man came riding to their door
He'd travelled far to be their wooer
He courted one with gloves and rings
But loved the other above all things
"Oh sister, will you go with me
To watch the swans sail on the sea?"
She took her sister by the hand
And led her down to the North Sea strand

And as they stood on the windy shore
The gold girl threw her sister o'er

Sometimes she sank, sometimes she swam
Crying, "sister reach to me your hand
Oh sister, sister let me live
And all that's mine I'll surely give."

"It's your own true love that I'll have and more
But thou shalt never come ashore."

Ide made a harp of her breast bone
The harp began to play alone
The first string rang a doleful sound
The bride her younger sister drowned.

The company gasped as one. The harp continued to play and sing, repeating the song. Dark, heavy-bottomed clouds gathered. There was a clap of thunder in the distance.

William turned to Etain, eyes ablaze. He pulled his hand away from hers, and rushed away from the table, overturning his stool in the process. He was headed in the direction of the horse stable, Ide noted. William's parents rose and followed him without saying a word. The other guests from Foyle looked at one another helplessly, at a loss for what to do next. A few were regretful they could not dig into the feast laid before them.

"William! You can't possibly believe this . . . this . . . witchery! This is Ide's work; she's always been jealous of me! William, William! Where are you going?!" shrieked Etain.

William's pace did not falter as he strode across the meadow to the barn. Neither William nor his parents looked back.

"Daughter, can this be true?" Father's hand rested heavy on her shoulder. "Did you harm Ciara?"

"Father, I did not do this," said Etain. She gained her feet, and shrugged Father's hand aside. "Who are you going to believe, me, your firstborn child, or the trick of some ugly witch?"

Before Father could reply, Etain took off at a run, heading towards the woods. Thunder drummed the heavens again, and the clouds burst open.

Some women screamed, others tried to save the most expensive dishes of the wedding feast from the rain, and some herded children indoors.

The men gathered in a knot, shouting at each other over the sound of the wind and pelting rain. The harp played on.

"We should stop her!" cried one man.
"Yes, we need a magistrate!" said another.

"You can't simply take the word of a magic harp; there's witchery afoot!" said a third.

Father held up a hand. His voice was calm and steady. "Enough! This is my family we're talking about. We must get Etain and bring her home. I want to hear her side of things."

Father and the men set off after Etain.

The village women continued to rescue what food they could, then gathered up their children and headed home. The remaining guests from Foyle departed without comment.

The harp continued to play its mournful song.

The rain battered everything, and lightning flashed in the sky.

Mother, Ide, and Hugh held each other and cried.

Chapter Eight

Etain had been tearing through the forest until her lungs felt stuffed with hot coals. She paused for a moment to catch her breath and listen for the men searching for her. They seemed to be getting closer. *I can't let them catch me.* The rain was powerful enough to penetrate the forest canopy and turn everything into slick mud. They might be able to follow my footprints in this mud. She started to run again with no plan, just obeying the panic that throbbed in her breast like a second heart: get away, get away, get away from them. Her fine blue wedding dress was torn now, and muddy to the knees. She had broken twigs snarled in her hair, which hung in dull heavy wet ropes around her face. She knew she must look a fright, but she did not care.

She needed to get away from father and the other men until she could think of something to tell them. She needed to come up with some way to pin this all on Ide. *It was probably all Ide's fault anyway. Yes, I pushed Ciara into the water and drowned her, but that was just in self-defence of my married life with William. Probably jealous, Ide had put Ciara up to seducing William, the evil bitch. Both my sisters conspired against my marriage to William from the beginning. Maybe even Hugh was in on it, for all I know. They are all against me! I had to do what I did. However, could I be happy otherwise?*

The trees started to thin, and Etain could see the lonesome sea strand and hear the surf. It was empty of people today, since almost everyone in the village was at the wedding feast, but there were a few upturned boats and coils of rope that marked this as a place men fished.

She ran clear of the forest and toward the water.

138

"I see her. She's on the beach," rang the deep voice of one of the townsmen.

I won't be caught. I won't be caught. I won't be caught. I won't. I won't. Etain ran into the surf, not feeling the chill. She moved deeper into the water as quickly as the surf and her voluminous skirts allowed, and was soon swimming, furiously kicking her feet and stretching her arms in long strokes that carried her toward the distant lip of the horizon.

"Get her, get her! She's swimming," came the voice of another man.

Etain spared a glance for the men emerging from the wood onto the beach. None of them wanted to try swimming after her in the North Atlantic sea.

"Good," Etain thought, "They are cowards and shall not catch me."

She returned her focus to swimming as fast as she could, a very difficult endeavour in a corset and many petticoats. After a few moments, winded, she paused again, treading water, watching, listening.

She was far enough away from shore to hear the men's voices, but not their exact words. They had noticed the small upside-down wooden fisher's boats, and had divided into two groups. Each group was trying to right a fisher's boat and half carry, half drag it to the water's edge. She was too far away to tell if they had oars.

Etain swam with renewed energy for a few moments. I'd rather die that go back to . . . to that whole life. Who can I be now, with a ruined marriage and accusations hanging over me. Better I swim out as far as I can never to return. She found her limbs starting to slow, feet no longer furiously kicking, arms feeling weak. The weight of her waterlogged clothing was drawing her down. If I quietly tread water and stop splashing they'll have a hard time spotting me, especially as it grows darker. If I can just evade them until full nightfall, I'll be able swim back to shore and sneak away. She continued to tread water, her movements just enough to keep the tip of her nose out of the sea. One day I'll return to this village on a white horse, with rings on every finger and a handsome rich husband by my side, that will show them, that will show all of them.

She was still fantasizing about wealth and power when her face slipped underwater for a final time.

Chapter Nine

Father and the men returned an hour later, bearing Etain's body. There was ocean kelp in her matted hair.

"John, what happened?" asked Mother.

Tears poured down Father's face as he explained, "We could not find her at first. She was so fleet of foot. We lost sight of her early on." He blew his nose on his sleeve.

"But she left signs of her passage through the forest. We followed the bent and broken branches. When we finally found her, it was on the beach. She was already in the water up to her waist. When she saw us, she started to swim out to sea. It took us a while to find a rowboat and get it in the water. By then she was just floating face down . . ." said Father.

"Good," said Hugh, cradling the now-silent harp in his arms. The pure white bone of the harp glowed, and the strings gleamed blue-black as a raven's wing.

"Hugh! She was a sister to you, same as me," said Ide.

"No! Not like you Ide, not at all like you," he said.

* * *

Ide lived for the rest of her life in her parent's house, tending the chickens, brewing beer, making herbal concoctions for fevers and coughs. There were always rumours about her being a witch, but her brewing work was so valuable to the village, no complaints were ever raised against her, not even when she was old and hunched and grew a hairy wart on the end of her nose.

Hugh stayed in the family home with Ide and their parents, as he never married. When he wasn't milling grain, he could often be found on the bank of the river, sharing a handful of wheat with the swans there. The village gossips referred to him as "peculiar."

After Father and Mother passed away, Ide suggested to Hugh that they bury the harp with them, but he would not hear of it. He spent hours every night by lamplight, oiling and polishing it. The harp played its mournful tune every year on the anniversary of Ciara's death. No note could be wrung from it at any other time, try as Hugh might.

---

[1] Etain pronounced "EE-tane"
[2] Ide pronounced "EE-da"
[3] Ciara pronounced "KEE-ra".

About the Author

Chloe Cocking lives in New Westminster, BC, with her person. She is preoccupied with coffee. Chloe can usually be found staring out the window when she should be writing.

She is the author of *Blood Rain* (Filidh, 2017), an urban fantasy/horror novel, *Fables Fictions and Fantasies: A Compendium* (Filidh, 2018), a collection of short stories, and *Hector* (Filidh, 2019), a book of poems.

www.ingramcontent.com/pod-product-compliance
Lightning Source LLC
Chambersburg PA
CBHW060122260626
47160CB00005B/1989